SO-ARJ-535

VETERAN'S DAY

GeorgeAnn Jansson

ZEBRA BOOKS
KENSINGTON PUBLISHING CORP.

ZEBRA BOOKS are published by

Kensington Publishing Corp.
850 Third Avenue
New York, NY 10022

First Zebra Printing: May, 1996
10 9 8 7 6 5 4 3 2 1

Printed in the United States of America

This book is very respectfully dedicated to:

ALL VIETNAM WAR VETERANS

To those who made it and those who didn't,
With heartfelt gratitude,
I honor you.

AND

The song "I'VE ALREADY SEEN HELL"
Words and Music by my treasured friend:
J. J. Hoopert,
I salute you.

Acknowledgments

A special acknowledgment to my sweet baby sister, Roxanne, and her husband, Danny Pike, and his mother, Louise Pike, for extending such wonderful southern hospitality with several wonderful getaway weekends at the family cottage at Lake Tillery in Mt. Gilead, North Carolina. And Sis, don't forget our lonely MIDNIGHT run on the long, dark, deserted switchback roads to the Indian Mounds on Halloween where we scared ourselves silly.

One

"The kind of life I'm living
is not the kind I planned. . . ."

It was his ability or his life. Neither one was worth a damn at this moment.

The bullet wound in his arm twisted with each movement. He clenched his teeth. Feeling the heat of freshly rolling blood as the hole reopened, he swiped at it and continued his efforts to guide the skiff toward the bank.

Water gently slapped against the grassy shoreline. Low-lying fog hovered like other nights, in another country, long, long ago.

Above him, atop the sparsely wooded hill, bright lights from a warm and cheerful cottage mocked him. The smell of wood smoke made him want to be home. He nearly laughed out loud. He had no home. No haven. But he would create one.

Jumping through the tall reeds and horsehair grass onto the embankment, he pulled the flat-bottomed boat behind him and snugged it to a tree. He tore at the damp underbrush and soon had the boat camouflaged. In a hurry now, expectation strengthening him, he straightened up and looked above him. He wanted to be dry and warm and he was hungry. Two days without food and rest made even a sane man wild, and he had begun to doubt his sanity at daybreak this morning.

He made his way quietly up the wide redwood-stained steps to the back of the house. Security gates. Regular patrols. A lot of good it would do them when he had decided to come by way of the lake. Money must make people feel as if they were invincible. Well, guess what? He laughed to himself as he put his hand over the .38 he carried in his torn pocket. This was all that made you safe. Or dangerous.

He remembered the area well. He wasn't a man to miss details. He'd watched some of the remaining wedding party from a partially hidden cove a little way off. He'd been bleeding, aching, exhausted, and angry. But still he had watched and his mouth had watered as they ate, drank, laughed, and danced on that deck far off and out of reach.

He had picked this particular cottage after a few hours on the water checking things out. It was more isolated than the others. He had noticed the pontoon boat from the clubhouse area head in this direction with some of the wedding party aboard. He might have to wait them out one more day but at least he would probably find food and drink there. His previous years of security work on these grounds reminded him that hardly anyone lived there during the week. So what if someone was still there by the next day? He hoped they'd all gone back, but then again, he growled as he tripped and wrenched his knee, they might come in handy.

Closing his hand over the butt of the gun and sliding the stiletto dagger from his pocket, he took the last step onto the deck.

He smiled the grin of a killer in anticipation. He picked his way up the hill, slowly, carefully. There was no rush. In a way he was sorry it had to be her. In another way he was glad. She'd been nice to him in that rich, aloof princess way; when who he was or what kind of a man he was didn't matter to her any more than which pair of shoes to put on in the morning. Only a few more steps, a scattering of minutes, and that steel would be gliding through that long, smooth, milk-white column of her throat. Continuous passage over soft skin and on to the jugular. O-positive blood would lurch free. She would slide from his arms like liquid silver. Quickly. Quietly. No one would ever know the queenly touch of the lovely lady again. He would be the last to hold her in his arms. The final fingers that would brush across her soft, creamy skin. The last body that would press against hers. The last who would feel what a woman like this could do to a man. He would gaze into those beautiful brandy-brown eyes once more before they closed forever.

Mackensie Elliott slammed the book shut and dropped it on the floor. The embers were burning low in the huge full-wall fireplace. She moved to it and dropped another log on, stoking the dry wood with the poker. Sparks jumped and sang as they followed the path of air up the chimney.

She must have been crazy to accept her sister's offer to stay out here and get some much-needed rest before going back to New York. Alone. And with a chiller novel to keep her company, for Pete's sake.

Goose bumps covered her arms. She rubbed them away. The house was dark except for the small lamp glowing in the kitchen. If she remembered correctly, each room had a door that opened onto the deck. She fervently wished she had thought to go through the house and secure them before now. She should never have started reading the scary book. Especially not with her imagination.

A steady breeze whispered around the house, bringing a hushed chill to the moist night air. It was purely stupid to let a book and the fact that no one else was close by unnerve her. But it did.

Flipping lights on as she went, Mackensie drew drapes and tumbled locks. The old cottage creaked and groaned as she walked. The main steel-girder support beam swayed the tiniest bit as she went from one side of the house to the next. She heard the slight twang of settling metal. Funny she hadn't noticed that before.

Walking down the hallway, she veered right toward the master bedroom. Her reflection in the full-length mirror caused her to jump. Mackensie stuck her tongue out at the wimpy face in the glass and continued.

She went to the closet to pull the plastic bag over her bridesmaid dress. Swinging the door open, she jumped back when a pillow and some quilts slid down and out like an overstuffed scarecrow to wrap around her legs. Startled and then quickly disgusted with herself, she kicked the bed-clothes back in a heap and hung her dress above them. She pushed the door shut and snapped the lock. She had a fleeting memory of closets that used to scare her as a child. Foolishness. She moved to the bedside table and clicked the lamp switch on anyway.

The pine wood in the living room fireplace crackled and hissed. A rocketing spark caused her to jump again. Turning lights off in her wake, she moved back through the living room to the kitchen to remove the peanut butter and jelly from the cupboard and opened the last loaf of bread. Normalcy, she told herself as she slathered the bread with a thick layer. That would make her feel better.

Sandwich and chips on her paper plate, she flopped back in the chair, one leg dangling over the arm, and pushed buttons on the remote control for the television. The picture was snowy and full of static, but it was a comforting sound, reminding her that this was the 1990s and she was at Lake Tillery in North Carolina. Not the 1800s on the Scottish moors. Though, glancing outside, as she had when she pulled the curtains shut, she couldn't have sworn it. A heavy fog had formed over the lake. She idly wondered how good the phones would be if she had the need to use them.

Headlights from the road skimmed across the walls, making her feel a little better. The security patrol was driving by as it made its rounds every hour. She almost laughed. Almost. She hadn't quite shaken the feeling that someone was watching her.

With one bare foot propped on the bricked hearth, she set the rocking chair in motion. The sandwich, the dull hum of the newsman's voice, and the warmth of the fire lulled her. Mackensie let her mind roll back over yesterday's events. It had been a beautiful wedding even if a few of the words were lost to the occasional race of an outboard.

Mid-October sunlight had dappled through the remaining leaves, casting her sister and her new husband in comforting shadow. The pink and moss green of the attendants' dresses blended with the environment. Wearing her gown, Mackensie had felt sweet, charming, and Southern. That was something she hadn't felt before. In New York, when she was fitted in one of her many expensive business suits, the only thing she was allowed to feel was capable. Working as assistant to the director of a production company paid well, but she was beginning to feel used by her job, manipulated by the people she worked with. A change was coming, but she hadn't quite decided which direction it would take.

Finished with the sandwich, she leaned forward and pitched the plate into the flames. Mackensie watched as the color turned from orange to blue and back again, the white sphere curling and disappearing. Her glance fell back to the book.

Mackensie picked it up and studied the silhouetted figures on the front. The hulking, shadowy male figure held a knife menacingly over the lush female form. A plump full moon hung in the background and one long scarlet drop of thick blood dribbled down the cover.

Mackensie got up and repositioned the rocking chair to the other side of the fireplace so her back wouldn't be to the deck door. Then, shaking her head at her own stupidity, she opened the book and searched the page for the paragraph where she had left off. After all, she had sat all the way through the movie *Cujo* completely alone. She would read this book.

He appeared before her eyes out of nowhere. Spittle traced a line from the corner of his mouth down his grizzled chin. The scream was jammed in her throat. Her stomach lurched to her chest, forcing her heart to stop. He had said he would come for her. She remembered his words now. Now that it was too late. Beyond moving, she swayed. The rank smell of him enveloped her as he lunged and imprisoned her with his free hand. Turning her so his arm was around her throat, he took the fleeting moments to watch her half-exposed breasts heave and fall with each tormented breath she took. The flowery smell of her hair, as he brought her head back against his shoulder, seeped through him. She kicked and twisted and flailed out with her arms over her head to beat at him. His lips curled back in a cold leer. The feel of her body writhing against his fanned his satanic passion. For an instant, he wanted to cast her to the floor and fill her with himself, but then the need to see her blood, run his fingers through it, took hold of him. As she, at last, battled to draw in air and shaped her mouth to scream, a high-pitched feral noise, he brought the knife slowly down and . . .

The phone rang in the back bedroom. The jangling sparked her nerves, sending Mackensie's own heart lurching to her throat. Disgusted with herself again, she set the book on the end table and sprinted back to the bedroom to pick up the receiver.

He watched her through the narrow opening between the curtains that she had all but pulled shut in his face. She seemed to be the only inhabitant. He shivered as the cooling breeze wandered through his wet clothes. His bones ached. His head was splitting. The fire in his arm had leveled to an inferno. While she ran to answer the phone, he moved into action. Quietly, the razor-sharp point of the stiletto slipped between the door and the jamb and disabled the feeble lock.

Once inside, he pushed the door closed with no sound and pressed back against the wall. *God, the air smells sweet in here,* he thought. Drawing a long breath, he let the faint scent of her perfume fill his lungs. He let the pleasure of it seep through his entire body as he closed his eyes. Wood smoke mixed with the lingering tang of whiskey. It pushed aside the smell of his own blood, sweat, and the lake mud. Leaning his head back, he closed his weary eyes again and waited, listening to the easy sound of her soft, throaty laughter.

The phone tucked beneath her chin, Mackensie sat on the edge of the bed. It felt better to hear the sound of a human voice. Her sister giggled and Mac guessed that her new husband, Danny, was nuzzling her neck, busy airport or no. Roxanne went on to tell Mac that she should go downstairs and open the water lines. After the security guys turned on the water tomorrow she was to go back down and flip the fuse marked for the hot water heater. Yes. Yes. They had a wonderful flight and were now waiting to be taken to the point of departure for the love boat. In turn, Mac assured her sister that she was fine and, yes, she had the emergency numbers Roxanne had left.

Back in the living room, she told herself that confronting the door to the basement was nothing. She marched right up to it and . . . what was that smell? Dampness? Animal? Mud? It must just be old air from the rarely opened cellar, she told herself as she closed her hand around the doorknob and turned it quickly. Opening the door wide, she felt along the wall for a light switch. There was none. She looked at the wooden steps that disappeared into the dark abyss.

She remembered. A string hung from the ceiling at the bottom, on the landing. Stalking bravely down the stairs, hand groping in the air, she located the string and yanked on it. The bulb was of low wattage and it dangled, playing the light across the walls.

She quickly found the spigot and turned the handle. Mackensie glanced over her shoulder at the expansive glass doors that led outside, and ran for the stairs. Spooky. She felt as if someone were right at her back, a fingertip away. Snatching the string and yanking herself into darkness, she took the stairs two at a time until she reached the living room floor.

She slammed the basement door shut, popped the lock, and leaned her back against the door to catch her breath.

Who's here? her mind screamed.

Him!

Who? Who?

The killer . . . the psycho in the book.

In one split second, Mackensie looked to the book on the table, then rubbed her eyes to clear her vision of the image her overactive imagination had conjured up. She forced her eyes open wide and stared at the apparition dripping blood and water on the wooden floor.

Air, trapped in her lungs, hissed to get out. The blood in her brain drained to her toes. Her stare darted from the gun in one hand to the long, narrow knife in the other. This couldn't be happening.

"Anyone else in the house?" he demanded in a low, raspy voice.

The scream that demanded to get out crawled up her throat and ended in a growl.

"Are you alone?" the vision demanded.

Her head nodded up and down, all on its own.

"I'm not here to hurt you." He scowled, pushing himself away from the wall and slowly moving toward her.

She became aware of her hand on the doorknob behind

her. She turned it deliberately, her palm muffling the click of the released lock.

She looked ready to bolt. Or faint dead away. Or claw his eyes out. She was beautiful. Even in his half-dead state he didn't miss the mane of long brown riotous curls that hung over her shoulders. Breasts hidden behind a Hard Rock Cafe T-shirt were full and rounded and free of restraint. Her stomach was flat, her hips were small. Long white legs led from frayed jeans shorts to petite bare feet. He saw something flicker across her smoke-green eyes during his split-second appraisal and then saw her make a move to swing the door behind her open and escape.

Despite the pain eating at his entire body, he lunged. The hand that held the gun slammed the basement door shut, the other, with the knife, came up under her pretty, stubborn chin. Obedience was essential. The guilt shot up through him. So close now he could see the flecks of gold in her eyes, he was sorry. But necessity and the raw, basic need to survive drove him on.

Mackensie felt the taper of the blade. The skin at her neck tingled and nerves carried that sensation to her spinal column. His stale breath strangled her as he trapped her with his dark, cobalt blue eyes. The dampness of his body transferred itself to hers. She eyed the stubble of growth of new beard. This vision was real. The thought sunk into her as deeply as the blade could have.

She watched his lips move, only inches from her face as he warned her in his deep, gravelly Southern drawl. "I said I wasn't here to hurt you. But I will if I have to. It's your choice. All I want," his words were clipped and spaced, "is food and shelter for a little while. And a bath," he added as an afterthought, straightening up and pocketing his gun.

Right, her giddy brain sneered. *That's all. And after he rapes you and murders you, he can waltz out of here clean and with a full stomach.* She clenched her teeth together, hard.

Before she spoke, she commanded her voice to be level. It came out as a croak. "Who are you?"

"Thomas Justice Murphy. Get me a rope."

"Why?" She straightened and pulled herself to her full five feet, four inches. If she was going to get roughed up, she'd do it fighting.

"To tie you up."

Blinking, still trying to clear her muddled mind, Mackensie disagreed. "No."

Narrowing his eyes, he grabbed her by the arm and jerked her away from the basement door. He looked from his hand to the slim wrist he gripped tightly. There was defiance in her fist, but there was also softness, fragility. He didn't handle women like this. Resolve reared its head and he pushed reason and logic from his mind. Some things just had to be done. The real world didn't exist right now. Her long mane of hair brushed across his knuckles as she tried to pull her wrist from his grasp.

Opening the door, he pushed her down ahead of him. At the bottom of the stairs, he snapped her to a halt as he looked around. His fingers bit into her soft flesh, embedding large purple circles.

Thinking clearly now, she waited until he pushed her toward the worktable, obviously going for the coil of hemp hanging there. Then, jerking her arm free of his grasp, she dashed toward the patio door. She'd go through the glass if need be.

But he was quick, and even as she sensed his grimace of pain, she felt him upon her once more. She heard the knife clatter to the cement floor as he grabbed her by both arms and spun her around. Giving her a spine-cracking shake, he threw her down on the plastic sofa that was stiff from the temperature of the basement. With half his body pressed against hers, she trembled from the contained energy she felt as his muscles crowded hers in a clinch akin to that of lovers. He drew a fist back and seemed to catch himself only at the last minute. From somewhere in his brain, good sense surfaced. He drew his fist down. Realizing she lay beneath him, that her breasts pressed against him, her eyes wide and wildly frightened on his, he paused. He wasn't this type of man. He was a good man. An honorable one . . . and then the survivor in him was back. As if cold water were poured across hot glass, his emotions cracked. He put his fingers deliberately and tightly around her throat.

"I don't want to hurt you. Don't make me." Fatigue washed over him. He was tired. So damn tired.

"Quit fighting me," he snarled.

Mac could see the warning in his eyes, feel the desperation and determination in his body. His shoulders were broad, the muscles there and in his chest steel-hard. Beneath her fingertips, she felt the strong beat of his heart. Was he deranged? Was he despairing? He was lethal. Of that, she was convinced.

As he dragged her from the sofa, her feet brushed the knee of his pants and she felt the frayed slices of denim and watched speckles of blood dot her bare foot. He was hurt badly . . . in several places. She didn't struggle as he yanked the rope around her wrists, clamping them in front of her. She watched, as if in a dream, as he looped the other end around his hand, giving them four feet of rope between them. After he picked up the knife and slid it into his muddied pocket, she reluctantly allowed him to shove her up the steps ahead of him. Mackensie heard the soft click of the lock as he secured the door behind him.

He moved quickly ahead of her toward the huge kitchen that curved off the living room. The tables and countertops were still strewn with bowls and plates of food. He grabbed a handful of pitifully small sandwiches and stuffed them in his mouth. He instantly felt a little strength seep into him. Darting for the sideboard, he grabbed a half-full bottle of red wine, pulled the cork with his teeth, spit it out, and knocked the bottle back.

She stared as he gulped the remainder of the sparkling burgundy down his throat. His eyes were wild. A hunted animal. His movements were sure as he stalked around the kitchen, jerking her around after him, like some mangy mutt on a leash.

He scarfed up a bottle of Jack Daniels and walked to the living room. Slamming the television off, he plunged them into a very loud silence. He strolled over to the radio and punched it on. Kenny Rogers cried over a woman. Satisfied, he shoved her into the rocking chair and let himself fall back on the couch. He sipped from the bottle of whiskey. Now that he wasn't on the run, watching over his shoulder, feeling the threat of being nabbed at any minute, he let his muscles go lax. Resting the bottle on his thigh, he took the time to examine his prisoner through sleepy eyes.

His gaze scanned her body and then came back to catch her own direct stare.

She glared back at him. The rope was starting to chafe her wrists. Her temper was beginning to seep through her fears.

He needed sleep. But first he wanted to bathe and clean his wounds. He looked back at her. She was still staring at him with green, defiant eyes. Damn it. He almost felt sorry. His thoughts were beginning to stray. It was a bad sign. He had to stay in control or she'd find a way to conk him over the head and his link to what he needed would be gone.

"You're going to sit on the john tied to me while I take a long, hot shower." He almost laughed at her indignant stare. "Then you're going to bandage me where I'm cut and then we're going to sleep. I'll tie you to the bed but I'll always have a hold on this rope. You make a move and my instinct, when I'm asleep, is going to be to stop you. I warn you not to make any sudden moves."

Hating his words, despising his thoughts, he pulled his gaze away from her.

She watched him, gauged him. He was examining every inch of the room he could see from where he was sprawled. She looked at his pants where the knees were torn, as was the flesh beneath. He was soaked with lake water to his thighs. His shirt was torn at the sleeve where a bullet had punched a hole. Buttons were missing, exposing a solid, hairy chest. A cut on his temple had stopped bleeding. Thick, unruly hair dipped across his forehead. An area around his jaw was turning dark purple. Dirt covered him from head to toe.

"There's no water." The sound of her voice breaking the silence surprised her and caused him to jerk his gaze back to hers.

"What?"

"No water. The best man forgot to have it turned on. We had to haul a little up here. It's in the kitchen in the twenty-gallon urn on the sink." Hoping this would make him anxious to leave, she added, "They're coming by tomorrow to turn it on."

"Who?"

"The maintenance men. In the morning."

"Christ." He wiped a weary hand over his face.

Fear scrambled around inside her. She fought to keep her voice from sounding like she was pleading. "Let me take you somewhere. A motel. I'll drive, you hide." *And when you least expect it,* she repeated in her head like a litany, *I'll scream my head off and people will come running from everywhere to pound you into the ground.*

Two

*"Another town—another bar,
Another hope—another scar . . ."*

He studied her, really looked for the first time. She sat straight, regal, and defiant in the chair with her hands tied in her lap. She was linked to him by the rough umbilical cord of rope. For one split second, he felt sorry for her. Hell, he felt sorry for himself.

But not for long. He stood up and jerked on the rope, forcing her to follow. They walked down the long, dark paneled hallway. He glanced into each room and then chose one. The master bedroom with the big round bed.

What next? her mind screamed. *What now?* She looked from the bed to him and back again.

He pushed her onto the bed and looped the hemp through a curl in the oaken headboard and back around his hand. Sitting on the edge, he worked his shoes off, yanked the patchwork quilt cover down, and crawled to the other side of the mattress.

"You might as well lie down and sleep. You're not going anywhere for a while," he muttered through half-closed lips.

She heard the exhaustion in his voice. She didn't move, but her mind spun like Rumpelstiltskin's straw through the spinning wheel.

He had his back toward her. Muscles strained at the

seams of his torn and dirty shirt. His breathing leveled, and Mackensie swallowed as she realized she'd been holding her breath.

"What's your name?" he mumbled.

Thinking he was asleep, she was literally jolted by his words. "What?"

"Your name?"

"Mac."

He turned his head slightly and then rolled over to look at her.

His hair was too long. It curled over his collar. Meeting his eyes, she was appalled that she was thinking how handsome he might be under all that dirt and blood. And how hard his body felt next to hers.

"What kind of a name is Mac for a girl?"

"Mackensie. Mac." She studied the wall in front of her.

"Mac and Murphy." He rolled back over. "Ain't that a damn hoot. Get some sleep. You're going to need it."

She didn't even lie down. Uncomfortable, weary and scared, Mac sat back against the headboard and worked the ropes confining her wrists.

Her skin was pinched and rubbed raw. A small trickle of blood seeped down her fingers.

She could feel a very male aura that surrounded her attacker as he lay just inches from her. She knew, instinctively, that she shouldn't push him too far. The odd thing was that she sensed something more. Contrition. Remorse. Was that it? Was that what she sensed lurking behind the dangerous, steely glint in his eyes?

Resting her head back against the headboard, she let her eyes drift closed.

A storm built outside the window. Shadows danced across the walls, highlighted by the small lamp on the bedside table he'd left on. Her eyelids were heavy and she drifted in and out of sleep. She was terrified to make a move. Suppose he took it for her trying to break free and came up with that knife in his hand. Reflex could have him sinking that blade up to the hilt . . . had he already killed someone with it? The thought made the blood drain from her head. She squeezed her eyes shut tightly.

She had to get away. But how? Her swollen hands were not likely to pull back through the rope. She followed the line, saw it curl through the headboard, drop down, and then wrap around . . . his hand.

His fingers had relaxed just a little. The rope was loose. If she got up and yanked as she ran, she just might make it to the front door, unlock it, and . . . and then what? She needed the keys to start the car and they were in her purse. At this moment, she couldn't even think of where she had last seen it.

Hope. It gave her the strength she needed. Moving ever so slowly, she inched her way to the edge of the bed. Move, stop, listen. Slide, stop, listen. He groaned and shifted a little. But he didn't wake.

Thunder rolled hard, echoing in the sky. She jumped. A sudden wind battered at the window, and he rolled to his back. The rope slipped from his fingers.

Lightning streaked and the storm picked up tempo fast. It was now or never.

She waited for the next barrage of thunder. Lightning took quick aim and fired. The electricity went out. Her heart lifted. Maybe this was divine intervention. She sucked in her breath and made her move.

Blanketed by total darkness, Mac jumped from the bed. One swift jerk, and she felt the rope slacken. Running and pulling, she was free. She plowed into the tea cart in her mad streak down the hallway.

Her purse had to be in the kitchen. She grabbed it awkwardly with her hands tied together, dumped the contents, and felt for the keys. Her breath hitched, and the blood pounded wildly in her veins.

She heard hushed, desperate sobs jerking in her throat

as her fingers searched, frenzied, through the contents. The cold aluminum caught her fingers. She thanked God on her run out of the kitchen. She plunged toward the front door, her bound hands outstretched, the rope trailing like a cat's tail.

Flesh. Human. . . . Oh God, it was him! The room lit up for seconds as yet another voltaic surge arced across the sky. Her hands were on his chest. His eyes sparked dangerously as he grinned at her. The raging sound of the storm echoed in her ears as its intensity mirrored itself in the face of the man who blocked her way.

Adrenaline soared. Catching him unaware, she shoved him aside with strength she had never tested before. Desperate now, she charged through the rain and wind toward her car, a scant fifteen feet away. It couldn't be locked. It wouldn't be. There was no need for her to lock it way out here. She prayed silently. She'd gone too far to stop now.

He was on her in a heartbeat. He tackled her, and they rolled to the ground and down the slight incline. His face was close to hers, his breathing hard and fast. Their eyes locked. Hers frightened and defiant. His cold and exasperated.

She stopped struggling under him and it almost undid him. For a split second she was soft and pliant beneath him, her breasts pushing against him. Her full mouth was so close . . .

The storm drove over them. She kicked out, she punched, she clawed, and she screamed. Her knee connected and he sent a string of curses into the night air. She scrambled up, slipped, and clawed her way up again.

She felt a scream tear from her throat as he grabbed her ankle and dragged her down. Mud and dirt forced their way up her blouse, and a sharp twig ripped the soft skin of her stomach. He reeled her in despite her frantic attempts to scale the hill.

Her fists connected with his head. A sharp pain

wrenched its way up to her elbows as she rendered blow after blow.

Drenched and slippery, they wrestled. They rolled. His long, lean body sprawled across hers. Rain dripped from his face to hers. Pinning her with his torso, he finally got a grip on her arms and forced them over her head. With Mackensie subdued at least for the moment, he relaxed, using his weight to hold her still. His head came to rest above hers.

Murphy felt a swell of passion rise. In the midst of it all, his biology kicked in. Damn it. Hating this, despising himself, he stood up abruptly, yanked her up, and threw her over his shoulder. He grabbed the railing for support and moved back toward the house.

Mac slumped across his shoulder. He had her beat. There were no two ways about it.

Like two drowned rats, they sat on the living room floor where he dumped her.

Both breathed heavily and glared at each other through the dim orange glow of the embers in the fireplace. He pushed himself back against the couch and rested. She had guts . . . He admired that. She had clear eyes, hiding nothing. He liked that.

A minute passed. Two. "Candles?"

"In the kitchen," she hissed, rubbing her wrenched foot.

He took hold of her by the front of her blouse and pulled her face close to his. "Move and I'll knock you out cold." For one fleeting instant he wondered what it would be like to crush his mouth against hers. Passion? Curses ran through his head. He didn't have time.

She had no intention of moving. Not just yet. She was cold, muddy, and bruised. She looked up when the flare of a lighter caught the wicks of two candles set on the breakfast bar. In the soft glow, she could see that she had opened the wound on his head.

He reached up and brushed at the blood that threatened to cloud his sight.

"Take my car and get out of here." Mackensie was surprised that her voice sounded quite demanding.

Ignoring her, he moved to the sink and yanked a towel from the oven door. He scowled at her as he pushed the cloth against the wound. "Not yet."

If she was going to die, then the hell with it. She walked into the kitchen and shoved her roped hands out in front of her. "Untie me," she ordered, unable to believe her foolhardy bravery.

He merely turned and smirked at her.

"Now!" she demanded. "Look what it's doing to my hands."

His eyes locked on hers. Thomas Justice Murphy wasn't accustomed to being challenged. "You'll make another break for it."

"Again and again. You'll kill me and it'll be over, but untie these. They hurt."

He looked down at the dirtied, swollen mess he'd created and his muscles knotted. He wasn't this sort of man. Not normally. When he put his hands on a woman's body, it was to soothe, to excite, to relish. He had an off-the-wall inclination to go to her, to gently untie the knots, to bring her injured wrists to his lips. . . . His hand moved slowly toward his pocket. He pulled the knife out and released the blade. Click.

He held it in his hand. She was mud from head to toe. Her face was streaked where rain had run its course through the dirt.

She closed her eyes. He was going to slit her throat now and be done with it. Opening them again, she vowed to try to somehow turn the knife on him. She firmly planted her feet apart and readied herself as he moved toward her, ever so slowly.

Whoosh! He whipped the blade between her wrists and

the rope fell away. The relief was immediate. She rubbed, gently, to restore the circulation and then pushed past him to the sink. Turning the spigot on the urn of water sitting there, she filled a pan.

With her hands and arms submerged as far as they would go, she moaned as the water stung and soothed both at the same time. She washed some of the mud from her arms and face.

She heard him drop into a chair by the table and turned her head to look at him. For a fleeting moment, she felt sorry for the man. Something was definitely there, underneath all the rest of it. It stabbed through her.

She turned her head, whipping her unruly hair back behind her shoulder. "Toss me that towel."

Two seconds clicked by as he studied her. He took the towel from his wound and flung it at her. She pushed it under the water and felt her stomach go queasy as the water turned a dull pink. Wringing out the towel, she moved to him and stood before him.

"Are you going to kill me?"

He glared at her. "I said I wasn't." Hadn't he already said that?

"Rape me?"

At his snort and shake of his head, she dabbed the wet towel to his wound. What was he reduced to? Rape. He'd never even thought of raping a woman in his life. He hated that she suspected he would. Under any other circumstances, he would show her. He would run his hands into that mane of curly hair and tilt her head back. . . .

His quiet, his stillness nearly unnerved her. The wound needed stitches. She picked up one of the candle holders and headed for the bathroom. He grabbed her wrist in a viselike grip.

"Follow me," she commanded quietly. At this point, what would be, would be. The faster she dealt with him, the quicker she could get him out of there.

He sat on the john while she taped the wound shut with a good lump of gauze pressing beneath.

Her fingers were gentle, careful. Murphy wondered what her hands could do to him. Her hair smelled of shampoo and rain. He studied her midriff as she worked and noticed blood on her shirt. *Too bad*, he thought. *Too damn bad I had to meet this woman under these circumstances. Too bad I had to BE in these circumstances.*

"You've cut yourself," he informed her as he lifted the hem of her shirt. Skinned and bruised. By his actions . . . no, by her own, he rationalized.

She pushed his hand away, but he persisted. Taking the same wet towel, he gently dabbed the abrasions. She pulled back. He placed a hand on her hip to keep her still. "Let me clean this."

His hand was firm and warm; his face was near her breasts. Mackensie felt the heat of intimacy. What was this man really like? "I'll do it," she snarled.

Snatching it away from him, she pulled her shirt up a little and looked. It was only a scratch. She felt his steady gaze on her as she put things away. "What now?" she asked wearily.

"I need to sleep."

"So?"

"I'm going to tie you up again."

Mac saw regret in his eyes. Honest, true regret. Some more of her fear rose and whirled away like a puff of smoke. In every action, every movement, even though it was made to subdue her, scare her . . . there was an underlying chivalry. Yes, that was the word, she thought to herself, at once amazed. He could have punched her lights out hours ago. He could have snapped her arm or cut her with that damned knife. But no, he just very stubbornly and forcefully directed her to do what she was told.

"Why are you here?" She walked back to the kitchen, the candle lighting their way.

"It's a long story."

Mackensie set the candle in the center of the table. Resting her hands on the back of a kitchen chair, she turned to face him squarely.

"It's going to be a long night."

He studied her.

"If I asked you to help me, would you?"

His words took her completely off guard. "That depends." If he'd asked her that question ten minutes ago, she would have laughed hysterically.

He shrugged. "Right now I need sleep. Tomorrow I'm going to need your help."

"Did you kill somebody?" she asked quickly before her nerve dissolved.

He laughed low in his throat and then sobered. "No. Someone is trying to kill me."

Great, she thought. "And you decided to bring them to my doorstep," she said.

"Hardly. I jumped into the back of a pickup truck stopped at a light in Concord. I jumped out again when I recognized this area from years back."

That explained his torn jeans, busted-open knees, and split head. But what about the bullet hole?

As if reading her mind, he flexed his arm. "Police."

"You robbed a bank then?" Mac assessed.

"No," he replied, his fatigue catching up with him. "I said we'd talk in the morning."

"I don't want to be tied up again. I don't want to sleep in the same bed with you."

"Too bad."

A chill worked its way up her spine.

"At least let me get out of these wet clothes."

He nodded. Each took a candle and went back to the bedroom. She set hers on the bedside table and started to leave. At his rapid movement to head her off, she explained, impatiently, "My things are in the other room."

He allowed her to tilt the door to the other room a little to change behind it. He listened to the sounds of wet clothes being peeled from her body. He heard the soft whisper of a nightgown passing over her head. He involuntarily envisioned the delicate material brushing over her shoulders, her breasts, over her hips and down.

She swung the door wide, and went ahead of him to the master bedroom. In the faint white glow, her figure was silhouetted through the nightgown. Pulling the closet door open, she extended her hand and showed him the closet was full of men's clothing.

She turned around to face the wall as he unsnapped what was left of his jeans. In minutes he was warmer and drier than he'd been in days even if the pants were tight and the T-shirt snug. He motioned for her to get on the bed.

When she hesitated, he made a move to assist her, almost like a lover. She crawled into bed.

He was gentle, making sure there was clothing between her ankles and the rope. Trying not to dwell on the damage he'd done to her hands, he wrapped her wrists after pulling the sleeves down and over the chafed skin.

In minutes he was asleep beside her again. Mac relaxed a little. She looked from him to the rope that attached them. A lock of thick hair fell over his brow.

What was going to happen tomorrow? How had all this happened? She turned her head to look at him again. Yes, he was real. This was no nightmare. There was no chance she would wake up and he would be gone.

Her body ached beneath the soft material of her nightclothes. She yearned for a bath. One with water up to her neck. And bubbles. Sweet-smelling froth soaking her and soothing her. He grumbled in his sleep and turned over, his arm flopping across her waist and pinning her close to him. His chin rested at her shoulder. "Move the men out," he muttered. "Incoming!"

She didn't move. There was torment in his voice. What grief, what misery had this man experienced? What did she care? He was nobody to her.

She squeezed her eyes shut and wished herself on another planet. Sometime during the ensuing hours, she fell asleep.

Water coursed through the veins of the house. Mac sat straight up in bed at the sound before she recognized it. Her movement woke him and he grabbed the gun he'd laid on the nightstand. Instantly alert and ready to kill, he sat straight up.

"Whoa," she jabbed her tied hands out at him. "It's just the water. The maintenance men must be outside." Bright sun exploded through the curtains.

Then it hit him. He remembered every detail. Feeling her wrestling against the ropes, he rolled over and began untying them. "Go to the door and thank them so they don't suspect something's wrong. Don't try anything."

"Sure. They'll think everything's perfectly normal. I have twigs in my hair and my face is streaked with mud."

"You're just going to stick your head out the door and thank them. Wash your face first."

He stood behind her with the gun at her back as she swung the door open and called to the men just getting back in their truck. She wished she could simply lunge out the door and shriek at the top of her lungs, but his grip on her wrist was tight and the barrel of the gun hard.

The men waved and smiled and cheerfully drove away. She sighed and closed the door.

"You did good."

"Let me go. You're hurting my arm."

"Where are you going now?"

"To the basement to flip the breaker for the hot water heater. I want a bath before I get dressed."

"No tricks. I'm not a morning person."

He stayed close to her on her trip to the basement and back up. In the kitchen she filled the coffeepot and began to put the dishes in the sink.

He sat in the chair and rested his elbows on the table. The smell of the percolating coffee about unnerved him. He could almost taste it. Its mere aroma nearly strengthened him.

She plunked down a mug full of the dark brown liquid in front of him and turned back to fussing in the kitchen. He felt better with each sip.

"Water's hot," she announced. She headed for the back of the cottage.

"I wouldn't want to have to shoot you, but no one can know I'm here. Leave the bathroom door open." Would he really shoot her? Not in the heat of a struggle, but in cold blood?

"I will not. Follow me." She led the way to the room she had chosen earlier and showed him that the adjoining bathroom had no window.

"I'll be right out here," he said as he sat on the bed, his stiff knees objecting.

She gathered her clothes and went in, slamming the door behind her. The bath felt wonderful. She could almost forget he was out there. She lay back and soaked. She moaned as the water began to soothe the results of their wrestling match.

"Time's up," he grumbled. He could not sit there any longer and listen to the sound of the water whispering over her body. He pictured her lying back in the tub, her hair wet and curling over her shoulders.

"Not yet," she snapped back at him.

Forcing the images from his mind, he stood and rattled

the door. "I'm aching, I'm cold, and I want the water. Now get out."

Mac left the water and dressed. She was certain the flush at her cheeks was from the heat of the water.

He liked what he saw. He may have been a hunted fugitive but he was still a man. Her hair was damp and curly. Her cheeks were flushed from the hot bath. She was wearing a pair of jeans that hugged her hips and legs. The hot-pink T-shirt dropped down over nice round breasts.

"Go back in," he ordered.

When she simply stood there and glared at him, he took her by the arm, picked up the clean clothes he'd fetched from the closet, and yanked her into the bathroom with him.

"Do I have to tie you up again?"

She scowled at him.

"I have no qualms about coming after you completely naked, so if you make a dash for the outside, I will come after you. And I won't be happy."

Resigned, Mac sat on the john and turned toward the wall. "Make it fast."

She listened as he shed his clothes, turned on the water, and stepped into the shower. Hearing his groan of pain as the water beat over his wounds, she stood up. His hand shot out from behind the shower curtain and clamped around her wrist.

She turned automatically and saw the real condition he was in. His broad shoulders were black and blue. The skin across his ribs was ragged. And there were old scars. Long, irregular, welted scars following the curve of his rib cage to his back. The hole in his arm was black and fiery red all around it. Looking down, she saw that his hip was bruised, his knees were nearly shredded, the cuts extending up his thighs. She pulled her gaze away.

"Either you sit down and wait quietly or I'll drag you in here with me."

God. What this man must have been through. Then and now. Naked, he appeared vulnerable . . . and tortured. Despite everything, she felt bad. What had really happened to him? She didn't care, she told herself. Why should she give a damn?

She waved his hand away and sat back down. She'd listen to his story. She conjured up a picture of a wounded and desperate wolf, one that if you treated nicely would be your loyal friend for life. The same wolf that would go for your throat if you crossed him.

Later, much later, he watched her as she moved about the kitchen preparing the meal she had promised. A pound of bacon sizzled in the skillet on the stove. Normalcy. Thomas Murphy wished that this was just what it appeared to be. A fine home-cooked breakfast between a man and a woman, after a night of lying together in the same bed.

They hadn't spoken since he had climbed from the shower and she had stopped him from getting dressed before silently handing him the tube of first-aid cream to apply to his scratches. She redressed the wound on his head. He had watched her wince as she poured peroxide on the bullet wound. Thomas Justice Murphy became slightly amused as she checked his arm for the exit wound and proceeded to pour the liquid in her hand to rub on it. She wrapped his arm with gauze and secured it.

He had sensed a change in her. She was still wary of him but not terrified. Maybe she would help him. God knew, he needed it. And that in itself grated him. He was a man who moved through life with no one's help.

"Toast?"

Her question derailed his thoughts and he looked up at her again. "Lots of it. Grape jelly."

Was that a hint of a smile he saw on her face as she turned back to the counter? Wouldn't that be nice?

"No grape. Just apple." She cracked four eggs in a bowl

and added a little milk. She poured the concoction in another skillet and whipped it mercilessly. Her mind flitted back to a morning, much the same as this, but it was her brother who sat at a table similar to this one. She was all of ten years old. He was twenty. She was fixing him breakfast. She had undercooked the bacon, burned the eggs, and the orange juice had seeds in it. But Austin had pretended it was the best breakfast he had ever eaten.

Why had she thought of that? Maybe it was because she saw the same intensity in this man. The same anger. The same bitterness. It had come along years later, but she remembered it. Vividly. She missed Austin. Always would. His death had been a dance of wastefulness. But no one had reached him. Not in time.

Murphy had to practically catch the sides of the table to keep from jumping on the food. She set a heaping plate in front of him and filled his coffee cup. Settled across from him, she watched as he dived in.

She nibbled on a piece of bacon, and studied him.

"What happened to you, Murphy?"

"After."

"After what?"

He pointed his fork at what was left on his plate. "After I eat."

So the man was starving. She'd bet he'd starved before. Mac saw him tense and relax again. "You're beat to a pulp."

He grunted and filled his mouth with more food and ate heartily.

The meal complete, he felt good for the first time in days. Full now, he pushed the plate away and accepted the refilled cup she offered him. Time to fill her in. And hope.

"I'm a builder. I was on my way to a job and my car broke down. I hitchhiked into Concord. I ate at a little diner while the guy at the gas station took his tow truck out to bring my car back in. He said the car needed some new parts so I hitchhiked the rest of the way."

At her doubtful glance, he shrugged. "I'm impulsive. Two men in a pickup stopped. They seemed like regular guys. Been drinking a little but there was nothing major. And then I saw the blue and red flashing lights."

He stood up, and looked out the window. "Before I knew what was happening, the driver pushed the pedal to the floor and we were being chased."

"Did you tell them to let you out?"

Murphy laughed and the smile transformed his face from handsome to heart-stopping gorgeous.

"Tell them? I was too busy clutching the damn dashboard to open my mouth."

He sat back down and sipped from his cup. "The police finally cut him off and he drove the damn truck up over the median strip and turned back toward Concord. Bullets started flying."

Talking about it now, hearing it aloud, reminded him. Something had snapped. At the exact time the first few rounds went off, he'd lost the ability to reason and his brain had clicked into automatic.

Three

*"While the folks in D.C. were playing games,
the big black wall was collecting names. . . . "*

"The driver lost control and slammed into an embankment. The blues were all over us. I was pulled out and spread-eagled against the truck. I started picking up some of the conversation then. They had robbed the auto parts store in town." He eyed her directly, gauging her reaction. There was none. Her face remained blank.

Shifting in his chair, he continued. "The three of us were under arrest for armed robbery. I said I was just a hitchhiker. The two men laughed and said that was a good try. The officer agreed. Three men robbed the store and three men were here in the truck. They even had descriptions of all of us."

"You too?"

"Look at me. I look like a thousand other guys."

No. He didn't. But she wouldn't comment on it. "Didn't they check your story out?"

"They already had my wallet. They were getting ready to handcuff me. No way in the world were they going to put them on me." She watched him absently rub his wrist. "It hit me. The hoods decided to say I was the other man to protect the real guy, wherever the hell he was."

Fresh anger drilled through him. If he could get his hands on them now.

"They were going down and taking me with them. It was that simple. I shoved the cop, grabbed his gun, and was off and running." Mackensie didn't miss the keen, far-off look that flitted across his eyes.

"I was hell-bent. I outran them. I hid for hours, moving constantly. They wanted me real bad." The sound of the sirens, coming close, moving away, whining, always whining. Filling the air, threatening his life. His body and mind had snapped into overdrive. Alert to the point of hearing his pores open and close. Like Nam.

"You would have been cleared."

"With those guys saying I was in on it? I can't take the chance. I was in prison in Vietnam for seven months. I was twenty-three." He remembered that as though it was yesterday, instead of long ago. "Nobody's going to lock me up again. Ever."

"Okay. Go on." Prison. Vietnam. The old scars. She began to see him in a different light.

"I hopped in the back of a pickup stopped at a light. I didn't care where it was going. At that point, if the cops had spotted me, I'd be dead."

"Meaning that you wouldn't have let them take you alive. For a robbery charge? That's a little strong, isn't it?"

He looked at her as if she must be demented not to understand. "Robbery. Resisting arrest. Police have a real aversion to anyone relieving them of their weapon."

She shrugged. He was probably right about that. "You mentioned before that you recognized the area. You used to live around here?"

"Charlotte. I was married for a few years and we lived there. I worked security for a while here. I went north after the divorce and started over. My brother had bought thirty acres of prime woodland in Remington, Virginia. Asked me to help him clear the land and build him an A-frame. In exchange, he gave me ten acres to build my own house. That's where I live when I'm in the state."

"Can't I call your brother to help?"

"No. I don't want him involved. They'd nail me to the wall in a courtroom. I'm not taking the chance. Besides, those guys ticked me off."

That was probably ninety-nine percent of it right there. "Where do you live most of the time?"

"I don't like to stay too long in one place. I keep moving. I've been drifting from town to town for twenty years. Home base is the cabin I built."

She moved to pour them both more coffee. He watched her. Suddenly it was important to him that she believe him. Why? He could continue to force her.

"Doesn't sound like the ideal life to me. Don't you get lonely?" At his look, she forgot the question and asked instead, "How do you think I can help you?"

"Newspapers. We'll go into town and get some. And there's a certain store I want you to visit."

She got up from the table and retrieved her pack of cigarettes and some matches. "I was going to quit while I was down here."

She heard his sigh and moved back as he lunged over the table toward the pack. Yanking one from the pack, he struck a match and lit it. He saw her watching him as he drew the smoke deep into his lungs and exhaled.

She took her chair once more. Murphy lit her cigarette and she, too, inhaled and tried to relax.

"I don't know that I believe any of this."

His eyes darkened. "I don't lie."

"Says you." When he tensed, she sensed she was pushing him too far.

What better way to put an end to this? She had other things to do while she was here. "So, you want me to visit a store."

She was going to do it. There was a hell of a woman inside that pretty package. He suffered another twinge of regret that he'd damaged that package. "The auto parts place that was hit."

"Why?"

"Talk to the help. See if they can describe the men. The third guy. I have to find him so I can clear myself."

She heard the hope in his voice and her heart went out to him. She reeled it back in. "Why don't you just hightail it out of here?"

"They have my wallet, my license, my description." Anger and desperation creased his brow and darkened his eyes. "They have an APB out on me, I'm sure." He drew on the cigarette again. His head snapped up. When had he realized something else was nagging at him? When had he paralleled all this to Nam?

"What else is there?" she asked. When he simply stared her down, she persisted. "Is there more I should know?"

His mood changed abruptly. He chose to ignore her question. He was in charge here.

"Let's get started."

The ride to Charlotte was quiet. He looked out the window, watching this way and that.

Wanting to help and not fully understanding why, she smiled. "Relax. They won't be looking for you with a woman."

He nodded but didn't take his eyes off the passing landscape. Down-to-earth worry had set in. Suppose he did get caught. He had dragged her into it.

Suddenly, he was back in the bush, hunted. He could see the asphalt road, the cars, the trees, but it was Vietnam again. He yearned to feel the reassuring weight of an AK-47. Every time he thought he'd shaken it, it came back. The car plowed through a pothole and he felt as if a grenade had hit close by. He almost waited to feel the dirt hit his helmet, cover the shoulders of his uniform. He was jumpy and he hated that.

Noticing, she offered. "Be there soon. Murphy?" His eyes held the look of a stalked animal for just a second but when he turned to look at her, it was gone.

"Be casual," he instructed her. He had to trust her now. "Don't draw any real attention to yourself." Any man would look twice at this lady.

She braked in front of the store and Murphy turned halfway in the seat and hunched his shoulders.

Reaching behind the seat, she pulled out a Redskins' baseball cap and plopped it on his head. At that moment she wished, fervently, that she could take these circumstances and twist them into something, anything, else. And then another, different kind of anger set in. He had shoved her around and hurt her. Why should she give a damn about him at all?

Instead, she simply touched his shoulder. "Stop being so jumpy. I need an air-freshener anyway."

He watched her walk into the store and browse. He didn't like her being that far out of reach. Was it only because she could simply take off running and leave him there, or was it because she was becoming important to him? The way she'd touched him just before she got out of the car. It was a touch of reassurance. Kinship.

Inside the store, she pretended to examine the new neon door handle strips, the triple-blade wide plastic wipers. She surveyed her surroundings and the man coming toward her. From under the bill of the hat, Murphy sat up, alerted, when the man from behind the counter left his station and approached Mac.

"Can I help you find something?"

"Not yet," she smiled at him.

He was grinning at her through tobacco-stained teeth. He had grease under his fingernails and a real need for deodorant.

"Anything you need, you just ask ole Harry here. Anything at all, pretty lady."

"Thanks, I will." She turned her attention back to the wall of accessories.

Murphy sat straighter in the seat when he saw the man size her up from behind. The punk.

Batting her eyelashes and turning on her sweetest voice, Mackensie exclaimed, "Hear you all had some excitement in here the other day?"

"Sure did. Makes a man wonder if he wants to own a store or not. Times are getting bad. People will do anything nowadays." Grinning from ear to ear, he hooked his thumbs under his belt.

Mac turned to size him up again. He was probably forty. He was a few inches taller than her. Grizzled. Life hadn't shown this man a particularly good time. "Heard it on the news. They're still looking for one of the men, aren't they?"

He offered, eagerly, "They'll get him. Have his picture and all. He won't get far."

"What about the other two?" She lifted a Mickey Mouse air freshener off the hook and sniffed. Bubble gum. She wrinkled her nose.

She saw his dirty arm go past her and pull a different one from its peg. He put it toward her nose and grinned. "Now that's more suited to a real lady like you."

Lilacs? Hardly. She shook her head. She chose the one with the trusty pine tree pictured on it. "Have any fancy valve caps?"

"Sure enough. Over here."

She chanced a glance out the window to be sure Murphy waited patiently as she followed the man in the grimy blue uniform.

"Makes a girl kind of excited to know there's an armed robber on the loose." *I don't believe this junk is coming out of my mouth.*

"Doesn't scare you?"

"Sure." She flirted, openly. "That's what's exciting. Were you here? When it happened?"

He grinned proudly. "Looking right down the barrel of their guns."

She pulled the carded dice from the rack and looked them over. Black and white. Looked like the real thing. "Did you recognize them? Were they local boys?" she asked casually.

A deep voice boomed from the back room. "Harry, I thought I told you to restock the oil shelves. Oh. You have a customer." The surly man turned on his heel and returned to the back.

"Saw 'em clear as I'm seeing you. Course I'd much rather look at you."

And I'd much rather run through New York in the dead of winter, naked, but Mac simply smiled coyly.

They strolled up to the cash register and Harry jumped behind the counter. "Did you have to go identify them in a police lineup?" Lifting her eyelashes slowly, she wet her lips with the tip of her tongue.

"Sure. Hey. How about I tell you all the details over dinner tonight? I'm leaving in an hour."

Mac drew her wallet out of her purse. He keyed in an amount on the register. "One dollar. The dice are on me."

"Why, thank you."

"How about it?" he pushed anxiously.

When she seemed hesitant, he was quick to add, "The police have one theory. I have another."

She hesitated another second, sharpening his excitement. "Where is it? I can meet you there."

"Sandusky's. End of Elm. North. An hour?"

"Okay."

His grin returned instantly. "What's your name?"

"Mackensie. See you, Harry."

"Mackensie." Hearing him test the sound of her name on his lips, she swung the door open and made her exit.

She made sure she swung her hips as she sashayed across to her car.

She didn't like it when Murphy punched the door open for her and growled, "Why the hell are you walking so funny?"

"If you don't like the way I'm handling things, just get the heck out of my car and get out of my life."

He turned and faced forward. She caught the subtle ticking of his jaw, indicating that it was a real tough job to keep his mouth shut.

"We've got a date." She plugged the key into the ignition. "That slime ball said he saw all three. But I still don't know how you think you can find that guy yourself."

"What do you mean you have a date?" This might be more than he'd bargained for.

"Sandusky's in an hour for dinner."

He snorted. "It's a dive. You won't be safe there."

She braked hard for a red light. He grabbed for the dash and muttered something under his breath. "I'm not safe anywhere, it seems. Do you want my help or not?"

Murphy looked out the window and back again. "I need it." *And I need you.*

He steamed. *If that man touches her, if he so much as puts one hand where he shouldn't, I'll tear him apart.*

"If you don't come out in a reasonable time, I'm coming in to get you."

"Last night you were ready to kill me and now you're going to be my paladin? Save it." She stomped the gas pedal. He slammed back against the seat.

"By the way, I'd like to take your gun with me tonight."

He froze. She could almost hear the thoughts running rampant in his head. After long seconds, he pulled the .38 out of his pocket and slipped it into her purse. "It's double action. All you have to do is pull the trigger."

"Safety on?"

"No safety. Just remember, it's not on an empty chamber." He shifted back to his side of the car. "Let's get on out there. I'll check around and see if there's a place for me to lay low. Don't take any chances with that guy. Get what information you can from him and then split. And don't lead him on too much."

"He'd just be finishing what you started."

She drove toward Sandusky's.

"I know it's an off question, but why are you suddenly so willing to help me now?"

She wasn't sure or perhaps she didn't want to dig too deeply for the answer. "Your endearing personality?" *And I want you out of the cottage. Gone.*

"You're not scared of me?" He didn't want her to be. Not any longer.

"Scared of everything. But it's different."

Sandusky's was indeed a dive. A bright orange neon sign flashed against the sky. She dropped Murphy off across the street and parked the car at the end of the potholed lot. She hoped Murphy kept a keen eye on the door. If she needed to leave fast, she didn't want to have to look for him.

It was growing dark. Inside Sandusky's it was even darker. Smoke hovered near the ceiling. Fans merely stirred the gray swirls around the room. The tables were wobbly and stained with glass rings. The room smelled of grilled onions and scorched frying grease. She found a table near the front door away from the blaring jukebox and ordered a drink.

At a newsstand half a block away from Sandusky's, Murphy leafed through the local paper. The third column down on page four drew his immediate attention.

Two men who allegedly robbed the T & R Auto Parts store last Wednesday night have escaped. It is believed the two will join a third man who eluded police when the three

were apprehended after a high-speed chase through Con-
cord. One of the men worked at T & R Auto Parts three
months ago. All three are armed and dangerous.

Beneath it were three pictures. Murphy's was one of them, his name in capital letters beneath the photo. He felt the hair stand up at the base of his neck. Plunking a quarter down on the counter, Murphy made his way out of the stand and strode hurriedly down the sidewalk toward Sandusky's.

Harry hadn't even bothered to clean up. Mac sipped on her drink and cast him a sweet smile.

He grinned back and slid his chair around until he was next to her. "I ordered a couple of steaks and some fries."

Mackensie merely shrugged, sweetly and stupidly.

The waiter appeared, placing two greasy plates in front of them. A pitcher of beer was set in the middle and two milky-looking glasses beside it. Harry poured and then offered her the ketchup. When she shook her head, he nearly emptied the bottle over his dinner plate. He attacked his food as if he hadn't eaten in weeks.

Her thoughts flew to Murphy. *Where is he? Is he close? I hope he's peeking through the dirty windows.* She pierced the tough meat with her fork and began to saw at it with a dishwater-spotted, bent-tipped steak knife.

"You live around here?" he questioned between huge mouthfuls of food.

"Visiting. My sister got married Saturday. I stayed on awhile as sort of a vacation. I live in New York."

He sat back. "I didn't figure you for being from around here. There's something different about you."

She tried to relax and teased, "Yes. My accent."

"More than that," he said, as he slipped a rough hand over hers.

Drawing back, she smiled again. "Tell me about the robbery."

He sat back in his chair and gloated. "It was nearing closing time and I was getting ready to shut off the lights when these three guys came busting in and . . . you really do like this, don't you?"

So her avid, eager look was working. She really should be on the stage. When he leaned forward, she had to force herself not to move back as he whispered in her ear.

"After dinner we could go back to my place."

"Actually, I have an appointment in an hour," she said, checking her watch.

He ran a finger over the thin suede strip at her wrist. "Maybe tomorrow night then. Ole Harry here can show you a good time. A real good time."

God! She shifted in the chair and forced herself to continue with this. And she couldn't figure out why. Murphy was nobody to her and here she was putting herself in danger for him.

"We'll see. Now finish telling me about those guys." She put a fry in her mouth to keep from screaming and bashing him over his arrogant head with the plate.

"They clicked the lock on the door after them. I heard it echo through the store and I knew. I tried to make a dash for the back door but they were all over me. One of them shoved the barrel of a gun in my mouth." He paused for a moment and caught her quick intake of breath.

Satisfied, he continued. "Pushed me up against the counter and emptied the cash register. Then they jerked me to the safe and made me open it. A man will open a safe with a gun resting on his tongue."

"I guess so. Go on." A nasty feeling crept through her bones.

"This really is something to you. You must lead a dull life back in that New York."

Mac shrugged. "Nine to five and then home. The men

up there are so businesslike. I like the men here in the South. They're macho. And strong." She braced herself and reached over to feel the muscle in his upper arm. It was rocklike and she forced an amazed smile.

"After you opened the safe, what happened?"

"They clunked me over the head, but not before I fought like a pit bull. They dumped me out of the truck right outside of town."

"You were lucky." But Murphy hadn't been. No sir. "They could have killed you," she sighed.

Murphy itched to know what was going on in there. Cap pulled down low over his eyes, he made his way to the side of the building and tried to see through the dirty windows. Nothing. He couldn't risk going in. He glanced around to be sure no one was watching him and moved to the back of the bar.

"You wouldn't have liked that now, would you?" Harry lifted her hand to his greasy mouth for a kiss. Mac came close to losing her dinner.

"I sure couldn't have met you if they did." She hoped this would somehow turn out to be worth all this degradation.

Harry slid his chair even closer. "Tomorrow night, when we go to my place, I'll tell you more. Stuff I didn't tell even the police."

I can't wait. "Like what?" She opened her eyes wide and stared into his.

"Well, I know where they might be hiding right now."

"Hiding?" she felt a clamminess envelop her.

"Yeah. Didn't you hear? They busted loose from the cops last night."

Ice water drilled down her spine. "No. I didn't know that."

He grinned and winked at her.

He knew something. The ape. An inside job! Of course. But she had to find out for sure.

"Come on, Mackensie. Let's dance."

"Well, just one."

He took her hand and led her to a small cleared circle in front of the jukebox. "Just one's all it's going to take, baby."

You've got that right, she thought as she put her hand on his shoulder.

He pulled her against his body tightly, and they swayed to the music. He pushed his pelvis against hers and pressed his lips down for a moment to kiss her temple. He mistook her shiver of revulsion for one of passion. The music went on and on and on.

Murphy slipped down the narrow walkway, diving into the men's room when someone came too close. He shoved the door open slightly and peered out. He could just see them. Anger and disgust rose in him, darkening his eyes and strengthening his resolve to end this quickly. The sooner it was done with, the sooner she would be safe . . .

Relieved the dance was over, Mac hurried to the table and lifted her purse. Feeling the weight of the weapon calmed her a little.

Knowing that Murphy needed another day to recuperate, she took a chance on losing their lead. "I'd rather meet you the day after tomorrow. Where shall I meet you?"

Without blinking an eye, the idiot took the bait. "Here. I live in a trailer out back."

"Okay. When?"

"I'll be here around six. Anytime after that." He brought his hand up to cup her cheek.

Casting him a seductive, womanly smile, Mac headed for the door. *Keep cool,* she told herself, *keep walking.*

She forced her feet to walk and not run. But the urge was there.

The cooling air hit her in the face, she scanned the

surrounding area for Murphy. She wanted the relative safety of Lake Tillery and she wanted it now.

A police car cruised by. She opened the car door, panic rising in her throat. What if they had spotted Murphy? Where was he?

She started the car and pulled it to the end of the parking lot, looking this way and that.

"Damn you, Murphy. Where did you go?"

"Keep driving."

She nearly jumped through the roof of the car. Murphy unfolded from his crouched position in the backseat.

"Damn you."

Mad with himself but taking it out on her, he demanded, "Drive. Drive! There are cop cars all over the place."

Careful to stay to the speed limit, Mac drove out of town. "We're clear. You can stop lurking behind me. You scared me to death. When are you going to stop doing that?"

She watched in her peripheral vision and ducked a little as he flipped over the back of the seat, settling beside her. His voice was low.

"They've escaped," he informed her.

"I know." Her long nails tapped against the steering wheel.

"How?"

"Good ole Harry and I talked about it. He's covering something, Murphy. He indicated he might know where the men are hiding. I'm meeting him here day after tomorrow around seven. We're going back to his trailer to . . . to have a drink. It's behind that dive."

Automatic protectiveness snapped into place like a steel trap. His frustration finally took hold. Murphy slapped the newspaper onto the backseat. "The hell you are."

"What is this? You think you have sole rights to knocking me around? Look, I can handle myself. Besides, I think I can get him to tell me all we need to know before he tries anything. I'll have your .38 with me. It's the only way, Murphy."

"No." It was bad enough he had involved her. Now she was putting herself clearly in the way of a very different, very ugly danger.

Mac guided the car over the curvy road. "Yes. You pulled me kicking and screaming into this and now I'm going to see it through. And besides, the sooner you are out of this, the sooner I can return to my own life."

The hand he put on her shoulder was none too gentle. "You're going to do what I tell you. You're not going around that guy again. I'll sneak out there tomorrow night, and see what I can find out."

She scoffed. "Right, and let everything that has led up to this go for nothing. You going to hog-tie me to the bedpost again? I don't think so. I'm guessing he's the third man."

Murphy thought about that. "Could be. Or he knows them and has given them a place to lay low for a while. Maybe they stashed the money and have to wait to get to it. I can't figure why they would stay in the area otherwise."

"I'll find out day after tomorrow night. Meanwhile, *we* lay low and you get your strength back."

"I said no."

"I'm not going to argue with you. I'm going. And if you try anything, I'll call in the cops, the marines, and a well-trained Girl Scout troop and you can talk your way out of all this."

She squared her shoulders. She was tired, sick and tired of being told what to do. Besides, something haunted this man and had for a lot longer than since the day he'd hitched a ride. She felt it. Something between the two of them connected and she didn't understand it. Two thoughts warred in her brain. She wanted this man to be history. She wanted to help him.

She let the car careen around the next bend. As he swore and shifted himself off the door, she smiled. "You'd better be as quick as you are tough, Murphy. I'm liable to need good backup."

He muttered an oath under his breath and reached for another cigarette. The front of the car quickly filled with smoke. She opened the window a crack.

"You'll do this my way." The scent of her perfume reached for him as he turned in his seat. He had to find some way to protect her, now. "My way, do you understand?"

Mackensie let her tensions and frustrations out in a loud sigh. "You can be a hardhead. Fight them, Murphy, not me. God only knows why I want to help you anyway, but I do. Now get off my back. I'll be fine."

He scowled and pushed himself back against the door. "I should have dragged you down to the lake and drowned you."

Mac shivered in the darkness. Her fear of him, her distrust, had buried themselves under a deluge of other emotions, but those feelings were there, gnawing at her. The other emotions might prove to be just as dangerous. She wouldn't take the time to think about them right now. It was more important to get this done.

Four

*"If my nightmares were movies,
what a story they would tell. . . ."*

Glad to see the dark shape of the cottage looming from between the trees, Mac swung the car in front and turned the key. The silence was heavy. Murphy ground out his cigarette in the ashtray. His head ached. He was dead tired.

After casting him a semisympathetic glance, Mac pushed the car door open. Murphy followed. She moved to start a fire, balling up part of the paper Murphy had thrown on the couch. She heard him head for the kitchen.

He opened the refrigerator door. The least he could do was fix her something good to eat. He was certain she didn't get any decent food at Sandusky's.

He studied the pitiful contents of the refrigerator. The lady was all right. She had come through for him. Scenes from the night before flashed before his eyes and he felt guilty. At least he could do whatever was in his power to keep her from getting hurt. She deserved more. She was right. She deserved to be rid of him.

The flames caught and roared up through the chimney. Mac moved toward the back of the house and Murphy let her. The time for worrying every minute was over. He figured from the sounds that she was changing the linen on the bed. Then he heard the water running and knew she was bathing. A part of him that had been lost for a long time stirred.

He had grown so used to work sites, cold efficiency apartments, and the habit of suppressing his feelings that he let the sounds seep through him and bring him close to a comfort he hadn't felt for a long, long time.

He wanted her. It was as plain as that. She made him think of roses, wine, intimate dinners in dimly lit restaurants. Music. He would hold her gently in his arms, and she would sway against him. Look up at him with those eyes, and he would lower his mouth to hers. He must really be losing it to be thinking of her this way. It was the situation. It didn't take army intelligence to figure this one out. She was a beautiful woman and he was a virile man. Being thrown together like this would fool anyone's nature into thinking things might follow a certain path.

Sitting in the rocker in front of the fire, he watched the flames wave and dance upward. He had turned off the stove but two giant cheeseburgers waited to be consumed. His eyelids were heavy and his entire body relaxed. But part of him, that part of his brain that had seen him through Nam, remained alert and on guard. Half asleep when he heard a movement behind him, he jumped up, turned, and grabbed.

Startled, Mac screamed when his strong hand clamped over her wrist. "Let go of me! Good grief, I thought we were past all this."

Murphy snatched his hand away. He covered his embarrassment. "Don't ever sneak up on me."

"I was beginning to think you'd been replaced with an actual human being. Calm down. Mmmmm. I smell food. You cook, Murphy? How interesting. I wouldn't have thought it." Noticing he was already into the brandy, she poured a measure of wine into a goblet and brought the food in on a tray. She set it on the hearth.

Perched on the bricks, she handed him his plate and

let the warmth seep through her from the fire at her back.
She had dressed comfortably in black jeans and a white
cotton T-shirt but she didn't miss his appreciative glance.

She looked at him, wondering. She wanted him out of
her life. She wanted this to be over with. Then why did
she care that he was hurt? Was it just a woman's instinct
to want to soothe and heal? What else could be the crazy
reason for her sympathy toward him? Other than that he'd
been screwed over royally. "You ought to fill the tub and
soak your aching body."

He nodded. He should. He wanted to. But what if she
left the house, left him stranded?

"I won't," Mac offered.

He looked up at her then, his eyebrow arched questioningly.

"Sink that knife in you or get in the car and drive away."

He thought about her words and her ability to read his
mind. "Why not?"

"Isn't it enough that I said I wouldn't? You don't look
like you feel well at all. Your hand was hot when you
grabbed me." Setting the plate aside, she rose and laid
her hand against his forehead.

"You're burning up," she exclaimed, alarmed. "Either
your arm is badly infected or you caught a cold out on the
lake. After you take that hot bath, I'll have a better look
at your arm."

"It's probably just from sitting too close to the fire." His
throat was scratchy and the headache hadn't let up even
with the addition of the food. His arm ached like a son of
a . . . and if he were to tell the truth, his whole body was
failing him. But this was nothing compared to what he'd
been through in Nam. Against his will, he remembered.
Every tiny, rotten detail. The stench of the small cell that
was his hell for many hours, days, and months spiraled
through his mind and he was back in-country that easily.

Mac became instantly concerned. "You're pale as a ghost. Are you sure you're all right?"

"Yeah. Yeah. Don't nag." He dragged his concentration back to the present. The cheeseburger was good. The fire and her company were even better. He glanced up and saw her studying him.

After a few moments of companionable silence, Mackensie ventured a question. "Why haven't you ever married again? All these years and no woman has snagged you? Aside from everything else, you're a very handsome man."

He grinned at that. "Told you. No involvements." Murphy watched as she slipped a potato chip in her mouth and then licked the salt from her lips. He looked away. Quickly.

That didn't make any sense to her. "You want to grow old alone? You don't ever want any children?"

Something stirred deep inside him. "Why not?"

"I really can't believe you'd give up all you could have for fear of what you could lose."

He sipped the brandy he'd found in the closet. It fired its way down his throat. He didn't care what she thought. Who was she to judge him?

"I could tell you a lot of things you couldn't believe. And even more you wouldn't want to hear." His eyes lost the coldness as quickly as it had appeared. "So tell me, what's your excuse? You're not hard on the eyes. You're pretty smart." He had to laugh to himself. A man could get lost in a woman like her. Soft, gentle, lively little she-cat.

She squared her shoulders. "How do you know I'm not involved?"

He shrugged. "No ring. Besides, no man in his right mind married to you would let you out of his sight for days at a time. I sure as hell wouldn't."

She accepted his offhanded compliment with a smile.

Color rose to her cheeks as she found her gaze on his mouth, wondering what it would be like to receive his kiss. He wouldn't be gentle. She didn't think she would want him to be. Then, embarrassed by her silly fantasy, she got up to take the empty plates to the trash.

What was wrong with her? Thinking of him this way? He was a fugitive. A complex man with hidden and suppressed feelings. Once they were set loose, she wondered what he would be like. Turning, Mac took her seat in front of the fire again, this time pulling her knees up and banding them with her arms.

He continued to look at her. The soft glow of the fire surrounded her. Right at this moment she looked totally unable to do any of the things he knew she could do. She could fight like a wildcat. Beguile a stupid clerk at a store. Perk a pot of coffee while her life was being threatened. Not to mention what she could do with her fists and knees.

Pictures formed in his mind. He was reluctant to let her return to Sandusky's. Last night he was ready to do anything he had to do to prove himself innocent. Tonight, he was prepared to talk her out of going back.

"I'll go into town early and snoop around that man's trailer. Maybe I can get the evidence we need before you're supposed to meet him. You're not going to be alone with that slime ball."

"Really. I'm following through on your plan with or without you. I have a feeling those men are hiding in the trailer. I get one look at the three of them and I'm out of there. Straight to the police. They'll pick them up and it's over. I've already noted the tag number on the truck. It's that simple."

He shook his head. "Nothing is that simple. I said no."

"Look, Murphy, you're not in the army now and I don't take orders. You got me into this and I'm not backing out." *Besides,* she told herself, *what better way to be rid of him?*

"Would you have expected one of your comrades in Nam to have stepped out of things when the going got tough?" She stood up and paced the living room.

"Quit talking. You don't know anything about Nam, Mackensie." He didn't feel he needed to explain. There were no words to describe the way it really was. No one ever really wanted to hear anyway. The initial wave of resentment eased.

"Think again, Thomas Justice Murphy." She'd seen pain associated with Vietnam. More than she ever needed to see. "Did it ever occur to you that I know plenty about Vietnam?"

"No" came his gruff reply.

She was reluctant to get into it just now. She was getting angry again and didn't have the strength to waste on it.

He closed his eyes. He was so damn tired. How was he supposed to think when he was so tired? It was hard for him to stay awake. Floating in a dreamlike world, he heard himself say, "I mattered over there."

It touched her heart. Oh, darn it, he touched her heart. She walked over to his rocker, knelt down beside it, and laid her hand on the arm of the smooth maple. "All of them did. You could matter here, Murphy. You haven't allowed yourself to. I'll bet your men loved you."

"We all loved each other." His words came painfully and were heavy with fatigue and brandy. "They're all part of me. The fights. The parties, the tricks, the long nights, the blood. All still part of me. When I came home, everything had changed. Except me."

She knew about that, too. The feeling that the world had gone on happily without you, while you were laying your life on the line every day and every night for people who didn't even know your name. She'd heard all about the blessed half-relief of stand-down time. The adrenaline-pumping firefights, the ground sweeps . . .

She heard his breathing take on the evenness of a deep sleep. She watched the lines across his forehead smooth out, and the crow's-feet at his eyes disappear. The thin line his lips had formed now relaxed into fullness.

When he jolted fully awake a few minutes later, she jumped, her heart thudding in her chest. Lordy, would he ever stop scaring her?

His eyes focused on hers and he continued the conversation as if they had never veered off. "You're not going. I'll think of some other way." His lids shuttered down again.

"I can be just as stubborn as you. I'm going. As soon as he starts pawing me, I'll just pull out the ole .38 and stick it down his pants. If I scream, someone will hear me. We'll try it, Murphy."

The rocker stopped. He slept, warmed by the fire and lulled by a weary sense of relative safety.

Later, she stood beside him in the bathroom, scowling at him. "Okay, let me see that arm." Mackensie yanked away the towel he had draped across his shoulder. His skin was still warm from the hot water. Drops glistened in his hair. The minute she saw the expanding red area and the angry darkness surrounding the bullet hole she knew they were in trouble.

"Get in bed," she ordered and left him there so she could search the cupboards for anything that would work. Alcohol. Warm damp towels. He was nearly asleep when she returned to him. Sitting on the edge of the bed, she wrapped his arm tightly and tipped the alcohol bottle downward to let a small, steady stream trickle its way toward the wound.

When he roared, she knew she was successful. Though he fought to get up, she wrestled him back. "Lie back. Be still. The dampness and the alcohol will draw the infection out. If it doesn't, you're going to the nearest hospital."

He had stripped before getting between the clean, smooth sheets. Now, as he thrashed and fought her, the sheet slipped away. She moved to pull it up and her hand brushed across him. His struggles stopped.

Quickly, she dropped the sheet and became very interested in taking his temperature.

"No way," he said pushing away the thermometer.

"Oh, there is another way." Her grin was like the Cheshire cat's. "Put this in your mouth before I put it in your . . ."

He took the thermometer without a moment's hesitation. A few minutes later, she removed it. A hundred and five degrees. That scared her.

"We'll give it a little time and then it's town. We'll simply tell the police what we think and let them take it from there."

He grabbed her wrist. "No. I want these men myself." His eyes bored into her. "Promise me. I'll be fine after some more rest. No police."

She could end it. Here and now. As soon as he went to sleep, she could call the law. He loosened his grasp but kept a hold on her. It boiled down to this. One human being asking another for help. "I won't call the law."

Obviously relieved, he let go of her. The look of gratitude in his eyes was more than she could take right now. She busied herself playing Florence Nightingale.

His eyes were almost shut and her voice seemed to come to him through a long, softly lit tunnel. Her hands were gentle as she wiped him down with a cool cloth. He felt his body responding to her touch and didn't even have the strength to take control. Even in his state of misery, he recognized the unleashed need.

Fully awake, he would have held back. But fighting sleep and the feelings her hands were drawing from him, he reached up and tried to pull her closer. He wanted to feel the coolness of her lips on his. He wanted to lose himself in her and not think or feel anything but release.

She batted his ineffectual hands away from her shoulder,

and then her neck. His fingers brushed across her breast
and she grabbed his hand to put it beneath the sheet. Fire
erupted at the core of her. He was a man. She wanted him.
It was as basic as that. And as stupid, she reminded herself.

She reared back. He needed to sleep and she needed
to think, get away from this bed.

He groaned, reached for her one more time, the movement dislodging the makeshift poultice from his arm so
that the scars on his back were clearly visible. She bent
down to examine them. There were eight. Long and curv-
ing. What pain had this man endured? Bending over to
wrap his arm again, she felt the urge to run her fingers
over the scars as if to take away the memory he lived with.

He was dead asleep. He would never know. Extending
her index finger, she drew it lightly across his skin. His
back was smooth, the scar rough. What had done that? A
leather lash? Bamboo? What else had they done to him?
Her heart rolled over. It wasn't fair.

She hadn't known him long but she was a good judge
of people. And this man lying in this bed was a good man.
She was certain of it. But nevertheless, he had interrupted
her life. Made a shambles of her little vacation. She wanted
this over. All of it.

He was floating on his back in a few feet of water, the
waves lapping at his wounds. The sun glared against his
lightly shut eyes, warming him, intoxicating him. The seductive sway of the South China Sea was a woman, making
wonderful, unending love to him. Cradling him, running
cool wet palms over his chest, his abdomen, and down.

He was mesmerized by the gentle tickle of her movement across the bottom of his foot, the lick at his toes.
Enthralled when her cool moisture flickered along his buttocks and beneath his back. Fascinated by the silken flutter
of her at his ears, whispering, promising. His sun-warmed

lips curled back in a smile. He was gently rocked by the swell and retreat, the surge and the ebb. Warmth and quiet. Welcomed.

The deafening explosion of a Claymore mine split the peaceful silence. He jerked, submerging himself. Strangling on the burning foul-tasting salt water, he flailed to reach the surface.

Chopper blades ripped at the air. Machine gun bullets popped into the sand, spraying it skyward. Screams. Howls of dying young men being torn apart by shrapnel, being blown to little pieces by mines. Orders were shouted. By whom? He was the man in charge. These were his men. They needed him. Adrenaline skidded into his veins only to be slowed, impeded by his constricting arteries.

He was going to swallow the whole ocean and his laboring lungs would fill up and burst. He would die in the water rather than in combat. No! No way. Finally, with a burst of effort, he speared up through the surface, sucking greedily, pumping air into his lungs.

Dragging himself out of the water and onto the beach, he fought to wipe his eyes clear. His hand was covered with bright, sticky scarlet blood. And now it rolled into his eyes. His head was split wide open. He could feel the sun beat at his exposed brain. But he wouldn't let it be over. No goddamn way!

Belly-crawling, he worked his way painfully toward the tall grass. The sand was hot, scorching his naked skin. He fought against a force that kept everything in slow motion.

An air blast shattered his eardrums and flipped him over onto his back like a turtle.

Suddenly cast in a shadow, he thought at first a huge black balloon was hovering over him. It seemed to twist and dance overhead, the sunlight refracting all around it. Forcing his eyes open, shading them with his hand, he could finally see. It was a helicopter that floated above him.

The body of a soldier hung half in and half out. Blood gushed down the stub that was once his arm. His weapon, still strapped around him, swayed in the air. With one leg wrapped around the seat braces, he seemed suspended for a second . . . arms reached for him and missed. The body dangled, delayed, and then plummeted toward the beach. Murphy rolled. The body landed within two feet of him without a sound. He closed his eyes and opened them again only to be met with the two glazed orbs of death.

The distinct whistle of incoming soared overhead and reverberated along the canal into his eardrums, threatening to rip his hearing from him. After another snap of a machine gun, a man close by pitched forward and rolled to a stop. A dead stop.

"No more! No more," he roared. Numbed against the searing pain, he rolled over and over, stood and staggered from side to side and surged toward his weapon.

A severed hand lay near the gun, the fingers still moving. The sound of tank movement, the voltaic thickness of the air, the smell of blood, and the sounds of dying filled his entire being. He let a great war whoop fly from his gut and upward. In one final gigantic leap, he lunged, grabbed the M-16, rolled it into full automatic, and unleashed his fury on the enemy. Yea, though I walk through the valley of the shadow of death, I will fear no evil, 'cause I'm the baddest son of a bitch in the Ashau Valley.

Mackensie heard him from where she'd fallen asleep on the couch near the fire. The sound tore through her like tempered steel. It brought back memories of Austin waking up the same way, the other family members flying out of their beds, pulling on robes, and running to him. She knew the sound of nightmares.

She ran to him as she had run to her brother all those years ago, and pinned him to the bed with her body. It was the only way. He was yelling and thrashing around, throwing his arms back and forth. The bed rocked under the force of his nightmare. His legs kicked around, his knee catching her shin. A sharp pain stabbed its way up her leg.

She dodged and shook him both at once. "Murphy! Thomas! Wake up, damn you, before you kill me."

Her voice was lost to him as he fought. He struggled. She shouted. Grabbing for his hands, she threw herself on top of them.

He went dead still. His chest rose and fell heavily. He opened his eyes, slowly. So heaven was where he ended up after all. An angel. No wings, but beautiful hair falling over her shoulder, and eyes . . . eyes a man could look into and be released from everything else.

She was a vision of sweetness and hope shining on him. And warmth. God, such fine warmth. He wanted to wrap himself in it. Let it thaw the ice he had let grow inside him. Then waking fully, he groaned, angry with himself. She moved to slide off the bed. His big hand shot out to stop her.

She turned to look at him, not wanting him to see the tears that threatened to fall. "You almost broke my arm, you big galoot. Are you okay?" she asked, her heart breaking a little.

He nodded his head and closed his eyes. "Now I am. It wasn't you I was trying to hurt."

She knew.

As his hands fell away from her, she sat next to him on the edge of the mattress. "Nam?"

When he didn't answer, she did. In her mind. PTSD. Post-traumatic stress disorder. She knew the statistics. Double the number of men killed on the battlefield have died since returning home.

Mackensie had lost an uncle to Nam. And lost her brother later on. She knew a lot about delayed stress. She remembered the time she had walked into a VA center and picked up the brochure. All neat and packaged. It was then and only then that she had partially understood the reasons for Austin's death, ten years after Nam.

Problems with concentrating. Difficulty falling or staying asleep. Outbursts of anger. Distressing recollections. Nightmares. The sense of reliving the experience. After having experienced events outside the range of usual human experience, one reacts instinctively to protect oneself.

She sat beside him. It was the only thing she could do. She could never claim to understand, merely to accept. It was too late to ever fix what they'd done to Murphy.

He was absently playing with a strand of her hair that wisped near her ear. It was soft and real and kept him grounded.

She knew being hunted again must be running through him like a bad movie, Vietnam sliding into the reality of this mess with the police.

She had been to the Wall. At first all she could do was look down at it, from a distance.

A reverence hung in the air. She had paused in front of the statue of the three soldiers, looked up at them, and then stepped forward to touch them. It was as if they were real. The three of them, standing there on the incline, looking off into . . . what? Home. They couldn't see her.

An odd, occasional splash of color—a flower, a flag, a pair of boots, a letter, a picture or two—jumped from the shiny black gash slit into the earth. Moving closer, she had examined the letters, laid her fingers against the cool, slick etchings . . . the names . . . so many names. She read many of them, repeating them over and over in her mind. The letters, the scratchings, were once men. Flesh and blood. Laughing, joking, prank-playing human beings who hadn't deserved this. And she felt the pride in them swell her heart.

Moving slowly, Mac had watched the sun's rays waver over each precious name. She saw her reflection cast against them. Life was the shadow there. And she remembered feeling the anger, the frustration, the injustice of the way the vets were forgotten by so many for so much. She had watched the slow-moving mourners pass each other, going in opposite directions. Only a few words were spoken. And they were not consoled.

All she could do was offer the veterans her pride in them, her appreciation, her undying loyalty. And now here was Thomas Justice Murphy. She would care about him. Even if she didn't want to.

She sat on the edge of the bed, afraid to show him sympathy, an emotion that she suspected would be tossed back in her face. "Better now? Can I get you a drink or some coffee?"

"I'll get it."

"No, you won't. It's no trouble." She left him then and walked into the dimly lit kitchen.

He'd have to settle for instant, she thought, as she turned on the hot water tap and let it run. Spooning the granules into two cups, she sighed wearily. What a mess.

Murphy moved into the bathroom and splashed cold water over his face. Why was all this coming back now? It seemed to always be there. Just beneath the surface. And after all this, she was being kind to him. He hated it.

Five

"You don't have to hold it in;
go ahead and tell. . . ."

He lit two cigarettes and handed her one.

She sat back against the headboard, knees drawn up and banded with her arms. He lay close, propped on one elbow. He drank from the cup of instant coffee she'd brought them.

She looked at his hands and pictured them wrapped around a hammer. And then a gun. "Do you build houses or what?"

"Some houses. Specialty homes." He stretched his aching body and rolled to his back, setting the coffee cup on the nightstand. "Projects mostly."

Genuinely interested, she asked, "Like?"

"Museums, complicated bridges, suspended and long span, playgrounds, castles."

Delighted, she smiled. So this man wasn't even close to what he appeared to be the other night. "Castles?"

"One so far. Maine. A seaport. This old guy owned half the shoreline. Struck it rich, I didn't ask where. He wanted to give his wife of forty years the dream she'd always had. So I built them a castle, complete with turret and moat."

Mackensie pictured it and sighed. "And of course a fire-breathing dragon."

"No, they took care of that. They had the meanest dog.

He had one hell of a growl. He'd wait until I was twelve rungs up a ladder and there he would be, teeth bared at first and then a constant I'm-gonna-get-you bark." His spontaneous answer, his easy tone of voice, gave her yet another glimpse into his well-hidden interior.

Pushing her hair back from her face, she challenged him. "Bet you had him eating out of your hand before it was over."

"Naturally," he agreed, drawing on the cigarette.

She didn't miss the weary way he ran his hand over his eyes.

"So you worked on big projects that took a long time. You stayed in the city or town until the job was done. You aren't home very often, are you?"

"Pretty much. I like it that way. I get to travel, put my hands to building something that will mean a lot to someone. Something that will be here a lot longer than I will. It's a satisfaction."

And a means of keeping himself aloof from the world. No ties, no responsibilities. Mackensie understood and envied him his freedom, to a point.

He was sleepy. She could hear it in his voice, see it in his body as he stretched and relaxed against the mattress.

"Do you have a lot of nightmares?"

He blew a steady stream of blue smoke toward the ceiling. "Doesn't everybody?"

"No, Murphy. Not like that."

He mashed out his cigarette and turned toward her, his eyelids lowering a little. His body was sore and aching. Resting a hand on his forehead, Mackensie could still feel the fever raging. She slid from the bed and pulled the covers over his shoulder.

"I think you need to sleep again."

Somehow, looking so different from the man who had pushed his way in here, he asked, "Since you're here, Mac, why don't you just stay awhile."

He wasn't pleading. He wasn't begging, and he damn sure wasn't asking. But the feel of her, the sweet scent of her took the outside world away. And he wanted to give back. Whatever he had inside that was good or decent, he wanted to share with her.

She hesitated. She didn't share a bed with a man easily and especially not one she had known a scant twenty-four hours. But as long as all he was asking for was solace, she'd oblige.

She scooted down on top of the blanket and let her body rest against his.

The quiet sigh that escaped his lips was enough. He needed someone. And right now that someone was Mackensie Elliott. And it was the first time in her life that someone really needed her just to be there.

Her hair tangled with the crisp curls of the mat that covered his chest. Her skin was cool against his hot, tormented shoulders where the blanket left him bare.

She wanted to slide all the way over him. Feel the full-length of him, every inch of him. His chest, his stomach, his legs, all beneath her.

His hand, the hand that clutched her to him, moved. Just a little at first, as if testing what she would do. She stiffened automatically and he stopped. In a few minutes his breathing returned to that of one asleep and she relaxed again.

It couldn't be love she felt for him. She scoffed at herself. It was sympathy. It was empathy. How did anyone know what love is or when you have it? She squeezed her eyes shut tight. This feeling must be it. She couldn't figure out what else it would be. What happened to him, from now on out, happened to her.

Why love him? He had scared her half to death, threatened and endangered her since the first minute she laid eyes on him. Thomas Justice Murphy was a rigid man. Determined. Stubborn. Opinionated. But was also gentle. With a goodness about him he couldn't hide from anyone who wanted to see it. A kindness was built into him and fitted as well as one of his two-by-fours into a frame.

He rolled on his side, now encompassing her in both his arms, the towel sliding away from the wound. The smell of alcohol filled the room. She gently pushed the bandage back in place. As she did, her lips brushed across the skin stretched over his collarbone. It was a sweet taste. A male suggestion.

The breath quivered from her when he seemed to settle and his chin rested against the top of her head. His knee came slowly up and reposed against her thigh. It was warm and hard.

She let go. It felt so good. So right. She breathed deeply and closed her eyes. It couldn't hurt anything, lying here beside him like this.

They slept. Like Adam and Eve before the apple.

Early the next morning, Mackensie awoke with a start. The bed was empty. She pushed her unruly hair out of her eyes. Maybe he had decided to go it alone. At once regret and relief crashed and flooded through her.

He wasn't in the room. Padding barefoot down the hallway, she was instantly relieved to see him standing at the screen door, sweet, chilly morning air wafting over him. He had bothered to pull on only a pair of jeans. The sight of his battered body caused an ache in her heart. *See,* she told herself, *it's just that he needs my help. That's why I'm so full of strange feelings and my heartstrings are vibrating.*

"What are you doing? You should be resting," she scolded lightly.

"Look. Come quietly." He turned, his fingers to his lips and his eyes too bright with fever.

She moved to him. "Ohhh." Deer. Five of them. Four grazing on the berry bushes and one standing still as a statue, scenting the air for danger. Mist swirled all around them. The first strong sun rays filtered through, casting them in the eerie safety of fog.

"They're beautiful," she whispered, shivering a little.

He slipped an arm across her shoulders. She accepted it and was grateful for it.

"I love this time of the year. Most people like spring and summer, rebirth and hope. I like fall. The mysteries of dying and the coming back again, maybe a little more vibrant, with a little more knowledge. Look at them. They're looking right at us and they're not afraid. Amazing." She cast doubts, fears, and confusion to the wind as she leaned against him. They stood that way, still as the animals in the mist and belonging to the beauty around them.

Something startled the deer. They flagged their tails and were off down the hillside, veering right when they reached the waterline and disappearing into the dense woods.

His body was too warm. She turned to look up at him. He was taking a deep breath of the fresh new-day air. "All Saints Eve. Halloween will be here in a couple of days. I used to look forward to dressing up and being scared to death. Of course, those were during the days when it was safe for a kid to wander the neighborhood for trick-or-treat. Before the age of sickos and doctored candy. What did you do for Halloween?"

He was smiling. "Knock over outhouses, string toilet paper through the trees, scare all the fairy princesses and clowns. Run through the graveyards screaming like a banshee." They laughed and the sound of it shocked both of them. On the edge of everything else, there was still a trace of happiness. She had to move away from him. This feeling, the one that spiraled around her stomach and landed with a plop in her heart, was happening too often.

She left him standing there and returned with a warm shirt for him to put on. After handing it to him, she walked into the kitchen. "So you were one of those little boys."

"Yes, I was, and proud of it." He stuck his arms through the sleeves of the shirt, grateful for the warmth. Where had that young boy gone? The one who was happy and carefree. Meeting life head-on. Hunting, fishing, and just plain whiling away a good day next to a cold streambed.

"I should have guessed." Mackensie fussed at the counter, clearing the dishes and mess from yesterday.

She looked back at him. He was still standing there, leaning against the doorjamb. He was lost in his own thoughts. "You shouldn't stand in that chill air. You've already got a fever, Murphy."

How long had it been since anyone had cared enough about him to worry if he was standing in a draft? A smile curled his lips. He'd been so busy moving through life, he hadn't had the time to think about what he was missing. But he did now.

He joined her in cleaning the kitchen despite her suggestion that he rest. He needed to keep moving. Murphy felt sure that if he lay down, his body would give out. He forced himself.

After breakfast, they took a walk. Not a brisk walk, but a slow stroll down a dirt path they found. When his fingers found hers, she didn't question the action. They could have been just any happy couple out for a stroll instead of two people entwined, however unwillingly, in a web of danger.

Late afternoon, they sat on the deck, watching the sun turn the sky from orange to purple and then to red. Like an oil painting held too close to a flame, the colors melted and streaked, mixed and spread in slow motion.

All day Mackensie had watched Murphy. He was growing sicker. The fever wouldn't let up no matter how many aspirins she forced on him, no matter how much food she offered him. His plate still held half his dinner even now.

"I think you should get to bed, Murphy."

He scowled and looked over at her. "Do you always nag

so much? When you go back to New York, will you nag
your boss like this?"

Back to New York. She hadn't thought much of it since
he'd burst into the cottage. No way. She wasn't going back.
Ever. Oh, she'd have to go back and close the apartment.
Store the furniture. But she wouldn't even say good-bye.
She'd just go. She could never live a life so meaningless
and wasteful again. She had Thomas Justice Murphy to
thank for that lesson.

"New York is history. A memory. I don't know what I'll
do now." It depended a lot on him and how all this would
work out. "I might settle around here someplace. I love
the South."

When she rose, he took her hand. "Thanks for all you've
done." He brought her hand toward him and then dropped
it.

It shot through her like sparks, the promise of what it
would be like had he laid his mouth there. "Go to bed,
Murphy. You're delirious."

"Not yet."

She'd learned a lot about him today. Not exactly from
what he said, but from what he didn't say. He was intelli-
gent, easy to talk to about any subject at all, and he could
feel. There was a depth to him. One that might hurt if
examined too closely. He had a lazy smile that was endearing, a laugh that was contagious. And even though he was
nowhere near at his best, he was very, very compelling.

When he quietly mentioned that she might stay with
him again that night, she did. Mackensie didn't ask herself
why.

He was shivering. The bright morning sun speared into
the room. Neither of them had changed positions during
the night. Murphy was nearly unconscious with the on-
slaught of the fever. He was caught with a coughing spell

and she took that advantage to slip from the room and go for more blankets.

He was delirious. She wanted to scream for help but he didn't want that. She knew how badly he didn't. She had seen the evidence of all he'd been through to prevent it. If she could clear this up tonight, he would be in the care of nurses and doctors in a matter of hours.

She managed to keep him in bed all day. It wasn't hard. He was as weak as a kitten and not always lucid. Spooning hot chicken soup down his throat, she thanked whatever gods prevailed that someone had left some meager supplies behind. He choked and spit but she forced some of the liquid into his mouth. He cursed. She crooned, and doubled his dose of aspirin.

The beautiful warm, sunny day was quickly spent as she kept him dry and then sponged him down. An indigo bunting sang cheerfully outside the window as she fought to get more medicine down his throat, mopped up spilled orange juice and turned a deaf ear to the ravings of his disoriented mind.

She read to him, the sound of her voice seeming to soothe him from time to time. Once he seemed to settle and opened his eyes to look at her and smile. Dark circles shadowed his eyes. The constant grinding of his teeth while he slept proved he was not resting. At last he was still and unresisting.

It was finally time to get ready. Mac dressed to run, in black slacks that clung provocatively. The pink cotton lacy top followed her curves. The satiny black jacket just begged to be touched. But her shoes. Black running shoes would aid her escape. She spritzed enough perfume at her throat to send a fence post into a frenzy. She had to have control over the entire evening, and as long as she could convince that pond scum that he could have it all when she was ready to give it, everything would go all right. It had to. Murphy's life depended on it.

He started to rally a bit, but by the time he was fully protesting, sitting up and shouting for her to come back, she was scooting out the door. If he fell on his worried face by coming after her, at least she'd know where to find him. Checking that the .38 was still in her purse, she drove away, resolve growing in her mind.

By the time she was on the outskirts of town, her palms were sweating. It crossed her mind to alert the police. She snorted mentally. They wouldn't believe her. If all had gone according to plan, Murphy would have been hiding out within earshot. But it hadn't and she was alone. Mackensie didn't have to do this.

It didn't matter at this point. She always saw things through to the end. The fact that she felt more alive now than at any point in her life proved what soaring blood pressure, adrenaline, and pure, unadulterated fear could do for your body chemistry. Not to mention what that man, the one back at the lake, could do. And as strange as it might seem, to her or anyone else, she cared about him.

An irregular pulse-beat charged through her veins as she pulled into the parking lot at Sandusky's. Patting the solid, reassuring lump that the gun made in her purse, she opened the car door.

He was there. He must have been watching for her. Holding the door, Harry all but smacked his lips together as he took in her scent and admired the female lushness of her. "You sure look a sight tonight. Makes a man feel like a real man."

She had only a second to thank goodness she hadn't held up the .38 to check it before he took her by the arm and led her to the trailer. She whipped on what she hoped was a wicked smile. "Thank you, Harry."

At least he had showered and changed. And she wondered where he had stolen the designer after-shave. He certainly couldn't afford it.

Six

"Another job, another boss;
another try—another loss . . ."

Once inside, she was assailed with the smell of old blankets and stale beer. She smelled wet dog, but she didn't see one. The living room-kitchen area of the trailer was dimly lit. Dirty dishes had been dumped in the sink to clear the counter. In the middle of the warped table, he had set and lit a brand-new candle that protruded from an empty beer can.

Mackensie pretended interest as her gaze skimmed over the plaid and maple trailer furniture, the skimpy, nicotine-stained curtains with the gold rings attaching them to the rod.

He offered to take her jacket and she could feel his eager hands at her shoulders. "No, thanks. It goes with the outfit."

He ran his fingers down the length of material and rested then, on her hips. "Sure is silky. Feels cool."

Sitting, she disengaged him. As he moved to sit across from her, she thought she heard a rustling in the adjoining room. A dog after all? The other two men?

"I rented a couple of good movies in case you want to watch them after . . . after a while. It'll be nice having a woman here for a time."

He suddenly had the gleam of a cannibal in his eyes . . . and she was the main course.

"You lived here long, Harry?"

"Too long. My old man used to run a junkyard right out back here until the ordinances made him give it up. Not that I missed rooting around in that mass of steel to find parts for the customers. Hands were always cut and bleeding. He died, right over there on that old sofa some years back."

"Your mother?" Did she care about any of this? She couldn't believe she was even pulling it off.

"I don't remember her. He said she took off when I was four. Tell me about your place in New York." His eyes gleamed.

"Nothing fancy. It's high up so I can look over at the park, watch the people."

"I've seen New York. In the movies. I think I'd like it. Especially the nightlife. All those lights and the women. Whew! The broads there are classy."

It was too warm in the trailer, and the air seemed filled with stale smoke as if five or six people had lit up and smoked for hours.

"So," she pretended avid interest, "tell me what you know about those escaped robbers."

His eyes darkened and he sat back to pout a little. "You are an eager little thrill-seeker, aren't you?"

She tilted her head and answered, "I like to get right down to it, Harry. Now go on, tell me."

Mac's eyes widened on cue, her lips twitched into an appreciative smile as the enthusiastic Harry, once again, went over the gory details as if from memory. Like a well-rehearsed alibi.

"So, like I told you, those two escaped. But you know, there might be more I could tell you if I was sure you could keep a secret."

"Me?" she laughed. "I'm a regular 007 when it comes

to being cool. What?" *And I'll go outside and scream it from the rooftops.*

He scooted his chair closer to hers. At the first feel of his lips at her throat, she tensed but caught it and forced herself to relax and lean into him. "Now, Harry, you're going too fast. I like some things really slow."

Grinning, he sat back and devoured her with his eyes. Wondering which was worse, she felt completely naked.

He kept his chair close to hers and leaned forward. "You might just be the kind of little lady we've been looking for."

"We?" *Oh, Lordy!*

"A couple of friends of mine and me, we're planning on traveling all over the country. Maybe you'd like to come with us."

When pigs fly! "Could be. What was that? I heard something. Do you have a pet back there?" That would help explain the bad smell in the trailer.

"No, it's my surprise, but first I have to know I can trust you."

She looked up at him through thickened lashes. *You bet you can trust me. Depend on me to turn your rotten existence over to the law.* "Trust me."

He jumped up like a kid going for a candy bar. Opening the bedroom door, he stood aside, beaming as two scruffy men in T-shirts came through the opening.

Proudly, Harry announced, "These are my friends." He came close and leaned till his lips touched her ear. "The bad guys that hit the store."

What was alarm came out as pleasant surprise as she stood up and, eyes wide, exclaimed, "You're kidding?"

All three shook their heads in unison. She looked at each man and then to Harry. He grinned widely and introduced the two. The tall, skinny one was Turk and the short, dumpy one Sully.

"And me." He thumped his chest proudly, "I wasn't a victim like I told the police. I was in on it."

Bingo! "No," she cried incredulously. "You? You all robbed the store? Well, I'm impressed."

As if to prove it, one of the men went into the room and returned, his hands full of cash fanned out like a royal flush. "It's enough to get us started. This isn't all of it. We stashed the rest of it in that old car behind the auto parts store. In case anybody gets nosy." He flashed a childish lopsided smile her way.

Einsteins, all of them. "Aren't you afraid someone will come across it?"

"Nah."

Harry moved closer, drawing her attention back to him and pushing the other men a little farther away, casting them a territorial glare.

"As soon as the heat dies down around here we're going to hit the road. The police are so busy looking for the third man, they won't be looking for these two for a while."

"The third man?" She pretended to be confused. "You just said . . ."

"Sit down, you guys, and shut your drooling mouths. She's mine." They all sat and Mac pulled her purse off the table and onto her lap. The heaviness of the steel made her feel a little safer. And at that moment she cursed herself for not thinking of concealing a tape recorder. She could have gotten it all and headed for the police.

"After these two hit me to make it look good and left, they saw a hitchhiker. They picked him up. Don't ask me why, I guess they thought they were safe." He laughed. "The two idiots must have been speeding. They punched it and gave the cops the chase of their lives. But then the knuckleheads lost it and wrecked. Cops were all over them and figured right away they must have been the ones that robbed the store, especially since Sully here couldn't keep his gun under control."

"We almost got away." The semitoothless wonder bobbed his head up and down.

Harry grew impatient, quickly. "Shut up, I'm telling this."

He continued, relating the tale as if they were all children gathered around a campfire and he had a wondrous legend to tell.

"The stupid cops assumed the hitchhiker was one of the gang. And the boys here agreed." He laughed again. He was so excited, she waited to see him start jumping up and down on the kitchen counter. It was then she realized she wasn't dealing with a sane man. Looking at the other two, she wasn't sure that there was a complete brain between the three of them. And because of this riffraff, Murphy had nearly died.

Okay. Enough. Now, to get out of here and to the police. "Wow," she breathed. "Just like the James Gang." *Forgive me, Jesse and Frank.*

All three grinned and looked at each other with self-fabricated pride and great satisfaction. She expected no less.

At this point, Harry figured he'd entertained the lady enough. It was her turn to show him a grand old time. Anticipation sharpened his senses. She would be yielding and willing to furnish him with a good, long night's distraction. Her skin, where it lay hidden beneath clothing, would be soft and she was classy. Already he could feel the boys' jealousy literally dripping in the air. Let them eat their rotten black hearts out. "Okay, boys, beat it. The lady and I want to be alone."

Mackensie saw the unmistakable gleam of lust in Harry's glassy eyes. "No! I want to hear what it was like. The escape." She cast a plea for understanding with her flirty eyes. She needed time. A few moments to plot a way to make a damn good break for it. She smiled. Her jaw hurt from the strain of it.

Harry did his best to hide his irritation as both men began relating the thrill of exchanging gunfire with the cops. He watched the animation on Mac's face. He wanted this woman in his bed where he could taste her, feel her, and feast on that fine little doll. He hadn't had many fine things in his life. None actually. But he meant to have this one.

"So," the two continued, one voice falling over the other in dopey enthusiasm. "We're headed out soon. It'll be just like in the movies. Desperadoes."

Harry reached up to play with her hair. "And we're gonna let you go with us. You can even drive the getaway car. Don't that sound exciting?"

Holy smoke! She stifled the bubble of hysteria that rose in her throat.

Harry stood. Mac stood. The other two stood. "Time to go, you guys." Harry indicated with a jerk of his grimy thumb for the other men to split.

"Time for me, too, Harry. I'm sorry. I had something else planned for tonight." Lame. She looked at her watch. "I really enjoyed this and I'm so honored that you would consider letting me join your band of merry men. Tell you what. I'll take you to dinner tomorrow night and then we can go back to my place and . . ." *When hell freezes over.*

The two men looked at Harry, waiting for his next move. She could nearly hear the word "wow" in the air. She made a nonchalant move for the door.

Harry made a quick dive for her when her fingers closed around the doorknob. She jerked back, involuntarily, and his hand clamped around her wrist. "I really must go, Harry."

His fake charm immediately turned to menace. He'd take what she had promised. "Women don't do this to me. I let you in on me and my boys here, and now I want in on you. And I don't like a tease."

She turned the knob and hit the door with her shoulder.

It burst open to slam against the side of the dilapidated trailer. Her purse slipped from her hands and landed on the steps, spilling the contents. The steel from the gun gleamed in the porch light. The three men, realizing in unison that they had been duped, leaped into action. But she had surprise on her side. It gave her the few seconds' lead she needed to stay alive.

Snatching up the gun and her purse, she was down and away as swiftly and gracefully as a frightened doe. And with just as much adrenaline pumping through her veins, expecting to feel the skin-splitting punch of a bullet any minute.

Glad she had purposely parked the car in the out direction, she managed to stay two inches in front of Harry's hand, jumped in the car, and slammed the door and locked it. The three men plowed into the side of the car, all at once. Sweat popped out on her forehead as the car rocked in response to the men's powerful and anger-fed blows.

Harry glared at her through the window as he tried his best to shatter it. She saw murder in his eyes.

She prayed the car would start the first time. It didn't. The motor turned over but refused to catch. They were going to break a window any minute and she would be pulled across the jagged shards and torn to shreds.

Their shouting grew louder. Harry pushed his face close to the glass and growled, "You cheating Yankee. You ain't getting away from ole Harry." His subsequent blow to the side window almost shattered it. Time was running out of her hourglass as fast as sheer terror was building up in her brain.

"Start, damn you. Get going." The engine wheezed, sputtered, and ground again. *I flooded it. Cool down. They can't get in.* She saw one of the men turn and run and knew he was headed for a crowbar or a shotgun. Her heart pounded so loudly the sounds of the men drifted away as if into a tunnel.

Grabbing the keys again and twisting, her elbow pointing toward the ceiling of the car, she sobered enough to take her foot off the accelerator. The car purred into motion.

Mac stomped the gas pedal, the squealing tires spitting gravel and half dragging the men along with her.

She let up on the accelerator for a split second to keep from losing control and then stomped it again. The men fell off the car like so many fleas from a scratching dog.

She had to get back to Murphy. She'd get him in the car and check him into the hospital and then she'd go to the police. She could bring the cops here, to the trailer. The thugs would be gone, but it would prove her story. Especially when they found out Harry wasn't working for the auto parts store anymore.

Her heart was still trembling. It was close. Too darn close. She ran a stop sign, raced a caution light, and soon found herself out on the dark, deserted road to Tillery. Murphy would be happy she'd found out the truth for sure. Mackensie yearned to see the look on his face when she told him.

Headlights bore into the back of her head. She checked her rearview mirror. A car . . . or maybe a truck was coming up behind her fast.

She wet her dry lips with the tip of her tongue. Speeding up, she found that the other vehicle did too. She slowed. And so did it. It had to be them.

Now what? She was close to Tillery. Ten miles. But she couldn't lead them right to the cottage and Murphy. If she attempted to turn around and head for a police station, they could block her.

It was only a truck, she told herself, trying to put panic at bay. An old truck with bent fenders and peeling paint. Surely, she could outrun it, lose them, disappear into the patchwork of roads that crisscrossed the small settlement. It was her only chance. And she had one shot at it.

The speedometer needle rose. Seventy, eighty, ninety. They had dropped back but they were still there. Ninety-five. The road straightened out and she pushed the pedal to the floorboard. A hundred. A hundred and five.

They fell behind. The gates to Tillery were coming up on the left. With a little luck she could disappear on the back roads before they noticed she turned off.

It was the only way.

She didn't detect the glare of their lights behind her. She must be clear. She had to be.

Then she saw the truck. Their truck. A good way back but coming just the same. Without a second thought, she wrenched the steering wheel and sent the car swerving into a ditch, the lurch of the vehicle causing her to bump her face on the steering wheel. She tasted blood. She cut the ignition and the lights.

The door was jammed. She put her shoulder into it and pounded. Nothing. Dropping her forehead to the steering wheel, she fought the urge to give up.

Exasperated and terrified, Mackensie aimed both feet at the door paneling and kicked. Cool air rushed in when the door swung open. Mac fell out of the car.

Looking back, she could see nothing, but she felt them. They were gaining. She had to clear the area. She darted away from the car. Staying low, she ran through the brush and blindly into the forest.

If she had judged right, the cottage was only a little farther.

It was then that she heard the heavy, angry thud of truck doors slamming. And the muttering of curses and promises. They had found her car.

Seven

*"I don't drift because I want to,
I drift because I'm damned. . . ."*

A scream trembled on the edge of her lips. Mac couldn't lead them to Murphy. They had no reason to suspect he was in the cottage just up ahead. They had no reason to be here other than to kill her. So she'd have to hide and wait and pray she didn't have to use the gun.

Moving as quietly and quickly as she could, Mac pushed on.

The lights from the cottage came into view. Murphy was silhouetted against the kitchen window. Would the two recognize him if they got close enough? She deliberately veered to the left and down the hill. The voices of the chasers faded a little. They were having trouble in the darkness, too.

Her chin was an open scrape. The knees of her pants were damp. Her beautiful jacket was torn and bloody. The rain had started again. She groaned quietly.

The forest grew still, the sounds muffled by the steady downpour. She could no longer hear the frantic steps of the pursuers or hear their menacing voices. But she hadn't heard the door to their truck slam shut again either. The rain increased, bringing a cold breeze with it. She sat wearily under a tree, leaning against the lopsided trunk and watching the cottage above her. Little did he know the trouble she was in. The only way to keep him safe was to stay put. She saw him pass the window in the living room.

Her breathing slowly returned to normal. The men must have gone off in another direction. Maybe, if she could get in the house and get Murphy, they could run down to the car and get away while the assailants were still in the woods. Hope strengthened her. A foolhardy plan was better than none at all.

Slowly, she stood. Her foot had fallen asleep and a sharp pain shot up to her knee. She made her way to the cottage steps, taking them slowly like a cat on the prowl. She was exhausted, but she kept moving. Reaching the deck, she stayed on her hands and knees and crawled to the door. She stopped, listened, and, hearing nothing, bolted through the door.

Murphy swung around so quickly, the whiskey in his glass sloshed to the floor.

She was on him in an instant and he on her. He was brushing the wet hair from her eyes and trying to make sense of her babbling.

"They're out there. They told me everything. They were all in on it. I got away, but they followed me. They're out there looking for me. They mean to kill me, Murphy. Murphy! Do something!"

He was too glad to see her. Relieved to have her beneath his hands, see that she was whole and untouched except for the bloody scratches on her face and hands. And he was angry. What she had done was stupid, and he hated stupidity. But she had done it for him.

Murphy was dressed and seemed steadier on his feet. When he left her standing there and returned a moment later, Mac merely watched as he stripped her wet, torn jacket off and stuffed her arms into a dry flannel shirt. His eyes were dark and his teeth clenched. Pulling on his own jacket, Murphy opened the door and pushed her ahead of him onto the deck.

"Murphy."

"Quiet," he snapped. "Don't talk. I have the boat. We'll row across the lake."

He was taking over and she was glad. And then she felt him whip her around and crush her to him as his mouth fell on hers for a quick kiss.

"Give me the gun," he ordered. He shoved it in his belt.

Once down to the water's edge, together they tore at the brush that covered the boat and pushed it toward the water. It was then they heard the searchers rounding the corner of the cottage.

One of the chasers complained loudly, "Let's get out of here. This whole place is haunted. It's creepy."

"Shut up, stupid. it. Find her. I want her."

Murphy heard her sharp intake of breath and slipped his hand over her mouth. He whispered in her ear, "They can't see us. Be quiet." He'd kill them. Gladly.

They froze. Murphy held her close and she could feel the steady beat of his heart. In the middle of all this, it comforted her. She clung to him.

He moved and she followed. Up to her knees in water, she helped him launch the boat and they both climbed in. They let the skiff slide out, leaving the oars in their places. At that precise moment the clouds shifted and the silvery moonlight showered them.

"Shit." Murphy grabbed for the oars and started rowing.

A bullet smacked into the side of the boat and Murphy rowed harder. Survival instinct kicked in and Mackensie reached forward and yanked the gun from his belt. Holding it in both hands, she pointed it toward the dark shore and pulled the trigger. The force of it snapped her wrist, but she fired again. And again.

Bullets came flying again and one grazed Mac's forehead. Dazed, she fell forward, pushing an oar overboard.

Damn them. They'd hit her. How badly? Fury tore through him. Murphy grabbed for the oar, and as he did, he stood and sent the boat off balance. It tipped and turned over. He grabbed for Mac just as they went over the side.

They were only a few feet from the shore but the water was deep. Staying close to the boat, they held on to the upturned hull and dog-paddled. The gun sank quickly to the muddy bottom of Lake Tillery.

Murphy tilted her head back and tried to see how deep the wound was near her temple. His heart iced over when it flashed through him what would have happened had she been leaning a little more forward.

"Keep going," he whispered, "they're coming down. There's a cove around the next bend. . . ."

If they could get around the bend before the others made the shoreline, the attackers would have to climb up and around again to catch them unless they decided to take a swim.

The sounds of one of the men tripping and falling, tumbling toward the water, powered Mac and Murphy's strokes. They rounded the bend just as they heard the splash in the water.

Something slithered across her midriff and there was no way she could muffle the scream. Murphy shoved the upturned boat away from shore with a mighty push. It sailed out and away. Heavy now, clothes soaked, they crawled ashore, weighted down with mud.

"What now?" she asked breathlessly.

He didn't answer. He simply pushed her under some bushes and covered her with his body to protect her. She felt him reach down and pull the knife from his pocket. She caught the faint flash of silver from the moonlight before he slid the weapon under him and ducked his head into her shoulder.

He might stick one of them with that, Mac thought, as she fought to keep from getting up off the ground. But the other two would grab her. She felt hysteria building up as the footfalls of the assailants drew closer.

Normalcy seemed light-years away. To think that just a few short days ago she was cheerfully driving down Route 81, singing along with the Everly Brothers, windows down, her hair blowing free in the wind. Little had she guessed she was driving her way right straight into hell.

Sure they could hear her breathing, Mac shoved the back of her hand against her mouth. Murphy tightened his grip on her in reassurance.

He was ready to do whatever he had to do to protect this woman.

The men were all around them. It was a pure wonder to Mac that they missed her and Murphy.

"Get the damn truck. We'll drive along the shoreline. Go across the lake. That's probably where they'll head."

The footsteps had stopped and they were only yards away.

"Who'd you suppose the other person was?" one of the men asked breathlessly.

"Figure it out, idiot." Mac recognized Harry's voice. "We've been set up. The bitch is with the hitchhiker that you two picked up. They both have to die or we're done for."

"Die! I ain't in this for no killing."

"Shut up. Git back up the hill and bring the truck down in front of that cottage. I'm going back in there and look around."

Mac and Murphy waited until the last one was in the house and then they ran.

His body was fighting. He could feel it. The survival instinct that was so sharply honed in Nam kicked into gear. Along with it new sounds and sights. Now wasn't the time to let it take over, to let whatever visions still controlled him have their lead.

A branch snapped across her cheek, drawing blood. "Stop, Murphy. Stop. I have to rest."

He kept going, ignoring her whispered protests, half dragging her. Mac was his responsibility now. More than anything he wanted to stop, sit down, and pull her into the safe circle of his arms.

Together, exhausted, they tromped through thickets and over bushes, slipping on rocks their fumbling feet had dislodged.

Deeper into the Uwharrie Forest the two cut a path, she powered by fear and he by the knowledge that if they didn't keep moving they would be found. And he couldn't let that happen as long as she was at his side.

From time to time, they could hear the rattle and shake of the pickup as it clattered up and down the nearby roads, the occupants searching, probably salivating to get their hands on them.

The forest grew denser, darker, and harder to negotiate. They both came to a dead stop when the sound of a very large animal taking flight startled them.

Murphy put his arm around her. "Flushed a deer, that's all."

She wasn't so sure. She fell heavily and yanked her aching hand from his. "No more. I can't."

He slid down beside her and sheathed the knife. The sound of helicopter blades ran through the back of his mind. The thud of anti-aircraft missiles roared through his brain cells. He shook his head. Not now. Stop. No more. Why did his mind insist on bringing Nam? He knew why. His life was threatened once again.

What was it the shrink had said to him once? "You want to be there, son, because that's where you were a hero." Time had been his enemy. He had turned inward more and more each year. And when he saw people happy, laughing . . . he knew it wasn't in him anymore. He mourned for it and settled. Until Mackensie.

She didn't like being a hunted animal. Now that some of the fear was subsiding, anger set in. She heard Murphy mutter something and tilted her head up to catch the words. He was mumbling something about getting the men to cover and calling for reinforcements. *Not now. Don't lose it now, Murphy, I need you.* The stark, cold realization of it exploded inside her.

She stretched up and pressed her mouth against his. His lips were cold. His arm came up and circled around her neck. She needed to bring him back to her. She spoke quietly. "Stay with me, Murphy. You'll get us out of this. You didn't survive Vietnam to be killed by two-bit punks."

She felt his hand under her chin, his thumb trace her lips. A moment of peaceful closeness passed between them.

"Get up, kid. We've got a ways to go tonight."

She got to her knees.

The ominous blackness of an abandoned building loomed before them suddenly and darkly. The walls suggested secrecy; the roof promised respite from the rain. If nothing else, a safe rest for a while.

Two pairs of eyes, blessedly adjusted to the darkness by now, searched the interior of the one-room shack. Blankets were piled on a rickety cot. A few buckets were thrown here and there. A wood stove stood in the center of the shack, its pipe dislodged and listing. A table, minus one leg, balanced precariously to one side. No words were spoken. They both moved to make a haven out of hell.

Murphy cleared a space on the floor and Mac opened one of the old, damp blankets and spread it. Murphy slid the table over to the door and turned it sideways. He pushed debris aside and she smoothed the blanket.

Murphy chuckled quietly. "If they stumble across this place they'll think we're just a pile of old rags in the corner." Shaking his head, he picked up the bucket and disappeared out the door. Mac listened to his muffled footsteps as he headed for the lake, and she busied herself making a bed. He needed rest and she craved it. Desperately.

He returned, the bucket filled with water. After he set her down on the blankets, he dunked an old rag in the pail and wrung it out. Carefully, he wiped the blood away from her wound. He was relieved to find it superficial.

She took the rag from his hand and, rinsing it, worked at the dirt on his face, and the red, heated flesh around the bullet wound. "You should be in a hospital where they could pump you full of antibiotics and orange juice."

"And you should be basking in the sunshine on the deck reading a romance novel and eating chocolate chip cookies, the breeze playing with your hair." His fingers dived in to comb through the tangles of thick, silky hair, his hand coming to rest at the back of her neck.

Trembling, more from his touch than the cool night air, Mackensie searched his handsome face. She brought the wet cloth up. His hand closed over hers.

He took the rag from her and set it in the pail. From what little moonlight made its way into the shack, they could see.

They cleaned each other. His arms, her arms. His neck, her neck. Leaning forward, Murphy feathered his lips along her collarbone and down, opening first one and then another of the buttons on her shirt. "Are you sure you're okay?" His thumb gingerly tested the slash the lead had cut across the pale flesh of her forehead. It was bruising badly.

She nodded. No words would come. It would take too much effort to speak and the words would never be enough. Drugged by his slow and painstaking care of her body, she let her head fall back. He ran his hands down her legs and arms, checking for wounds as he explored the glory of her form.

A fog, heavier than the one outside filled her brain. Sounds disappeared. Only sensation remained. His rough hands feathered across her skin gently, with the movements of an artist dabbing oils over the canvas. His warm breath whispered at her ears as he brushed his lips across her cheek. His cool, hard mouth warmed as he ever so gently laid it against her own.

Her hands went to his solid shoulders, mindful not to stress the wound that smoldered there. Her fingers smoothed across his chest and up until her hands were on either side of his face, the tips of her fingers dipping into his thick, unruly hair.

Slipping her blouse over her head, he gently wrapped her in a blanket. They spoke no words. None were needed. This was the coming together of two people, two strangers . . . two souls who had known each other all of their lives and yet had never touched before now. Before now.

Kneeling, she reached out and unsnapped the closure of his jeans. He slid her cold, wet slacks down her hips. She tugged at his jeans and tossed them to join the soggy pile of clothing. They moved toward each other, closer. The pure wonder of the touching of two exposed bodies and minds opened hearts and souls.

Naked, exposed, searching, exploring, trembling, they touched. She slowly opened her arms, offering the blanket, affording him the invitation he looked for. She heard the slow, reverent intake of his breath as he reached forward and drew her solidly, purposefully, against him. Flesh pressed to flesh. At once, a threat and a promise.

Their chilled, bruised bodies touched, lightly at first. Anticipation raced through their blood. One hand warmed the other. One arm rode along the other. They moved closer, closer still. A little at a time.

Their eyes were open and searching the dark shadows for each other. His hands roamed her back, following the arch down her hips and buttocks. Her fingertips played where his hair touched his forehead, curled at his neck. She traced her hands over broad, hard shoulders and drifted to solid forearms. Her seeking mouth slipped across his shoulders, down to his chest. Tasting him, she licked at his warm flesh, kissed her way to his tightened stomach muscles.

Mac's groan of pleasure when Murphy pulled her tightly against him, and the feel of him, the knowledge of his eagerness, shimmered through her like moonlight on rippling water.

She ran her hands down his sides across sharp hip bones and beyond. His hands cupped her breasts and he let his thumbs brush across the rising peaks. He brought his mouth down to replace his hands.

He would have much preferred she have music and candlelight, flowers and sweet words. All he had to offer was himself, and all that made him Thomas Justice Murphy. The place would have to be what they made it. To him, right now, it couldn't have been sweeter than lying in the middle of wildflowers in the meadow.

They lay down together, she cradled in his arms. He kissed her breasts, the long, slim column of velvet throat. Dragging his lips across hers, he murmured, "You deserve better than this."

A sound of pure surrender escaped her lips. "Nothing is better than this." Her lips curved in a slight smile as she ran her hand down his rib cage and lower. Shifting so that more of her body was in line with his, she reveled at the sound of the sharp intake of his breath.

Murphy held back. His release could come swiftly, easily. He wanted her to cry out for hers. He wanted her to know every sweet sensation he could bring to her and more. His hands roamed, lingered, and explored only to stray some more.

He didn't want to move for fear the languid, hot anticipation her every touch brought him would fly away. Her kisses matched his, not gentle but taking, demanding. She moved until her body was on top of his and then her pace increased. She pressed against him. Her small hands played across his chest and hips and her seeking mouth left his to find his shoulder, kissed the inside of his wrist. Bringing her mouth back to his, she whispered, "You're beautiful, Murphy."

Her simple words jerked through him, snagging on the craggy depths of his heart, the one protected and jailed until now. Catching her ear with his tongue, he left a hot, moist trail back to her mouth, where his tongue darted to taste the flavor. Gently, he shifted, turned so that she was beneath him.

It was too dark to see, but he felt her eyes on him. No questions. Only trust. Dear God, she trusted him.

Her hand came up to trace his cheekbone and his mouth. "Make me yours, Murphy."

As she arched against him, knowing and wanting it all, he said her name and she was lost to him. Forever. And without regret.

The wonder, the anticipation of what was about to happen between the two of them, that they would be one, in body, in mind, in soul, wavered between them. She lifted toward him and he pushed, the entry as smooth and swift and sweet, gliding along to fill her.

They were out of control. It wasn't needed. Instinct guided them both. Never had either of them been wanted like this . . . and the knowledge that it could go on, be there whenever the desire arose, was freedom.

Racing higher and higher, the blood whirled in her head and floated each time he murmured her name. Power. Her hands, her own two hands, was all she needed to please him. To show him how much he meant to her. She had power she had never tested and it was exhilarating. She could give so much more than she thought possible. And it would only increase.

Her hands tugged at him, dragged over his hips and

buttocks and back again. Pressing hard against her, pulling back, ever so slowly . . . he would never get enough of her.

Rainbows arched and built behind her eyes, the colors floating, mingling, and brightening. His warm breath was at her ear, then flitting across her lips. His hard body, beneath her hands, was slick with passion.

He stopped driving her. Her body pressed toward his. He remained still. With all the power that was in him, he drew this moment out, to capture the pleasure she was offering him. And then control was relinquished as he began to move, slowly and then quickly. As he crushed his mouth to hers, he felt the ecstasy mount with a will all its own.

Building. Climbing. Skyrocketing. Each held tight to the other as a new and unexplored part of their universe exploded open and closed again, taking them away into the most beautiful region where there was only heat and glory and each other.

Eight

*"And I look to you for heaven,
'cause I've already seen hell. . . ."*

When Murphy woke several hours later, his first thought was *peace*. God, that's what he'd been missing all his life . . . and he hadn't even known it.

She fit. With her body curled against him, her hand rested on his chest. Daring to move his fingers only slightly, he slid them across the silky skin of her arm and then up to her shoulder, across her cheek. Yes, she was real. But how could the simple act of making love and having love made to him do this? And all that had led up to this, the looks, the awareness . . . he'd been with women before, lots of them. But nothing compared to this.

In her sleep, Mackensie moaned and snuggled closer to him. Her hand crept across his chest and down to his waist to tug him even closer to her satiny nakedness.

The thrill of possessing, of wanting and cherishing spiraled up through him, heating his blood. His thoughts turned toward her mouth and he wanted to feel the eager velvety softness again but he dared not wake her. She needed sleep.

Their ordeal was far from over. The first faint glow of dawn began to illuminate their cocoon. As he looked around, he saw that their surroundings were worse than he'd imagined in the night. And now, as the dark, painful memory of another hut pushed forward in his mind, he found, for the first time, it couldn't quite make it. Not with her so close. The image skulked back to the recess of his brain. Murphy's lips curled into a sly smile.

Her awakening was akin to the movements of a cat. He soaked it up, watching the slow, languid unfolding of limbs, the long, lazy stretch and arched back. A low purr in her throat preceded the slow upward sweep of dark lashes. She smiled, eased herself up, and touched those sweet lips to his.

His life had changed for all time. No matter what became of all this, he would carry forever the sensations she gave him. At what exact moment had he fallen in love . . . a thing he'd sworn to himself he would never do? He wasn't an apple pie and picket-fence man. He'd long ago decided that wasn't the type of life for him. And the fact that he kept moving, kept putting distance between himself and relationships that threatened to develop beyond casualness should prove it to him.

Now was enough. Just now. This moment. So far and away from anything he'd felt before. The ache, the anger he carried with him since Nam slid away to shadowy places of his heart and she filled him.

He was glorious. His naked body was hard, the corded muscles quivering as he moved beneath her hands. She lay over him, the cool morning air shimmering across their exposed flesh to mingle with the new-drawn heat of passion.

She turned her mouth to meet his and let him know how precious he had become. Even though the knowledge of it had streaked into her like lightning from a storm, she had absorbed it and grown strong from it.

His arms came up to band her to him. Her lips roamed his throat, his shoulders.

The light grew and expanded through the cracks of the lean-to, casting points of light in her eyes.

"Good morning," he murmured beneath her eager mouth.

She smiled against him.

She felt the stirring of his body. Sitting up, astride him, she let him catch her hands with his. He brought one and then the other to his mouth and kissed each one. Despite the fact that both of them were battered and bruised, the coming together eased them.

She shifted until their bodies came into alignment and then she slid slowly down, filling herself with him. When be began to rock beneath her, she gazed down at him and whispered. "Be still. Just for a little bit."

His eyes opened and locked on hers. She saw the fervor there, and felt him swell and tighten within her. She began to move ever so slightly.

Hands linked, bodies joined, they began the ritual as old as time. Each touch, each awakening, every movement echoed and brought them closer together. Taught them both what it was like to be cherished, to be loved.

She untangled her hands from his so she could run her fingers across his chest and down to where they became one. She saw pleasure flash as pain across his eyes. She smiled. Power. It filled them both.

She loved this man who was once a stranger and a threat. Now, just days later, he meant everything to her. Her life was his. No matter what happened from here on out, she would have this.

She was glorious. Her head tilted back and riotous waves of curls hung down past her shoulders. Her skin, sheened with passion, was perfectly beautiful. High, full breasts tempted him, promised him. She gave so willingly, so eagerly. She looked down at him with that belief shining in her eyes and there was nothing left to do but receive it. He was powerless against her conviction. Right now, for this small passage of time, he yielded.

He had wanted it to last a long, long time, but the man

in him grew impatient to the point of breaking. There would be more times. They would be like this, just like this again.

He turned her beneath him and continued his exploration of her face with his mouth. He kissed the gash on her head, his mouth gentle and healing. Again his body wanted to rush things but he held back, drawing out all the pleasure he could. She wrapped her legs around him and arched hard.

Her urgent and asking movements were too much. He faded into her, in and out of her world, her reality.

Alive. Vibrant. Pulsing. Mackensie had never known such loving. She pressed her lips to his shoulder and cried out his name.

She realized he wasn't there the minute she opened her eyes. Then she heard him near the door.

Turning to look, her eyes met his as he simply held out his hand. She got up and took it, pulling it to her lips for a kiss. Strong hands. Hands that would protect her, love her, and escort her.

His grin was devilish. "Follow me."

"Out there? It's cold. We're buck naked."

He nodded. "What better way to be?"

The edge of the lake was near. He guided her to it and together they slipped into the cocooning, closing water. "I've checked things out. It's safe so far. There's no sign of them."

The water was silky and a few degrees warmer than the air. She knifed under only to come up a few feet from him. His eyes were hot and hungry. She kicked the distance between them and reached out for him.

"Maybe some hairy monster lured them into his den and tore them limb from limb. He roasted them over a campfire and stored the rest at the bottom of a cold, running creek bed for later. Maybe he's picking his teeth with their bones right this minute."

She was a delight. She was fresh air after a year underwater; sunshine after months in a coma. She gave to him. Freely. And he wondered at the preciousness, the selfless openness of her soul.

He brought her against him and banded her lithe body to his. "You deserve satin sheets and candlelight."

She could picture it and planned on seeing to it that Thomas Justice Murphy had many nights in his future like it. But for now, she wrapped her arms around his neck and rubbed her mouth over his. "You're all I'll ever need again."

It wouldn't last. It couldn't. This feeling of coming home. It wasn't in him to stay. When the time came for him to leave, she'd understand. He'd see to it. And they would have the good times to remember and take along their separate paths. He couldn't ask her to spend her life with a man who would always be dealing with his own hell.

She knew what he was thinking. He may have moved on from everyone else he'd known. But he wouldn't leave her. Now or ever. It was too strong, too right, the emotion, the need, the want. She had always believed she would know when the right man came along. And she did.

Their slippery bodies lined up, accepting the gentle toss of the water, shoulder to toes. She smiled, her arms twined around his neck as they bobbed on the surface, their legs bumping occasionally as they dog-paddled. She murmured against his lips. "We should get dressed and see if we can get out of here."

Ducking his head to nibble on her throat, he answered, "We will. I'll bet they're still driving around. We'll go back to the cottage and call for help."

Shivering, throwing her head back to look at him, she teased, "Sure, now that we've nearly been killed, we'll go for help like I said from the beginning."

The vicious seriousness that clouded his eyes as he pulled back to look at her was bright. "I was wrong to put your life in danger along with mine. I don't want you hurt. I'm going to get you to the police. Then I'm going on alone."

She pulled him roughly to her. "No way, Murphy."

His hands played along her sides, brushed over her breasts, and, sliding down, found her. "If ever there was a woman I could live my life with, it's you."

"You're a fool, Murphy." The hurt cut through her. "Listen to me. You're not going anywhere without me, nor I you. I won't ever leave you alone again."

"Understand something. It's not your decision. Right now I have to concentrate on nailing these guys. With you here I have to watch out for you. Right now it's important to me that you're safe."

"You didn't think of that when you kidnapped me," she badgered him lightheartedly, pushing aside the small sting his words brought.

"You got the information I needed. If I hadn't been down, it wouldn't have happened this way. I've got to move on these guys now. It's a long shot but they might just light out of here. Then I can't prove my position."

The cold threat of reality tightened around her throat.

"I think they're too scared to leave us alive, Murphy."

He smiled. In some ways she was such a child. "Could be they'll decide to just put a lot of distance between them and the law here. That leaves me an escaped criminal. I don't like that."

She wrapped her arms around his neck and held him close. This living, breathing human being had been through so much.

All she had to offer him was relief. She would give him a buffer zone where he could relax and trust . . . and heal. She would keep him safe. She would provide the haven his weary soul needed. The love she felt for him strengthened her.

His hands were working magic on her, and when he shifted, lifted her, and settled her again, she was his.

Joined together, he floated them toward the shore where the water was only ankle deep. He was on his back and she was over him. Together they rode along with the lapping water, and even if he didn't know it, she knew they became united toward their destiny. A destiny of love and laughter, work and rest, long, lazy sunsets, evenings settled in wing-back chairs reading by the firelight.

For a long while, they lay there, linked together hand in hand, like two lost souls washed up on the shore after a raging storm. Shivering, she welcomed the first heated rays of the morning sun. She held tight to his hand. Together they presented to the world one force. One to be reckoned with.

Reluctantly, they returned to the hut. They dressed quietly, each wrapped up in thought. Scattering things back to their original disarray, they headed out. The trees overhead swayed with the warning of another oncoming storm. They were a long way from the cottage. She stopped beside Murphy, her hand in his, as he seemed to pause and use his senses to direct them.

Here the trees were huge and dense and dripping with moisture. They were immersed in the Uwharrie Forest. Mackensie shuddered and was grateful that she wasn't alone.

She paused when he did and followed his gaze. Hills and valleys, a far-off skyline, leaves and branches. "Damn if I don't think we're lost. I hate this."

Believing in him, totally, she shrugged. "Trust your instincts, Murphy. It's all we've got."

He led and she followed. Deeper, deeper into the forest but always following the shoreline from a safe distance. Spanish moss hung from the low-lying limbs to snap and grab. Mackensie swiped at them. What she had once found beautiful had now taken on a different meaning. She couldn't keep the creepy feeling away now. She was losing her bearings, and when the sun was high in the sky, hidden except for the most fleeting moments, she dropped to the ground, weary and worried.

"Rest," she pleaded. He slid to the ground beside her. "Tell me a story, Murphy. What was your last job? Where was it?"

When he looked at her as if she had finally gone around the bend, she explained. "The sound of your voice makes me feel safe. Talk."

"Ashton. Kentucky. Construction. We built a church. It's beautiful. It's old-fashioned. They shipped the stained-glass windows all the way from England. The old preacher, had to be nearing seventy, came out every day to look at it. Nearly every word out of his mouth was a quote from scripture. I grew fond of the old man. Sometimes we'd share a sandwich or two at lunch. Used to sit on an old tree that had fallen but somehow part of the roots had remained intact and the tree continued to grow along the ground like nature's own couch." Murphy laughed and shook his head. "For a man of his age, he had such aspirations. He'll never live long enough to see a fraction of them come true, but that didn't seem to bother him. My guess is, he's lived on illusions all his life. Wanted me to stay, help him around the place. Settle down. Attend church regularly."

She lay back and watched the sunbeams fight for entrance to the forest floor. "Well, I'm glad you didn't."

He arched his brow. "Are you?"

"Aren't you? We'd never have crossed paths."

He nodded and placed a sweet kiss on her lips. How could he tell her it might have been better for her if they hadn't? "I tried to explain to him that wherever I am is my church. People who are used to buildings can never understand what you mean when your heart, your belief, is your religion. I don't know. But I'm square with the man upstairs. We've had our talks. Anyway, the church completed, I skipped out the night after we got our final pay. It was better that way. No good-byes." He didn't tell her about leaving the offering. Somehow it suited him to be the first to donate a few dollars to help the old man see some of his dreams come true. The first being a fanciful organ. One of the big ones that nearly pitched you out through the window when it was fired up.

Mackensie ripped at the huge leaf she held in her hands. "And after your trip to help your dad, then what?"

"A new wing on the children's hospital in San Antonio."

Mackensie sat up, her eyes bright with fond memories. "I dearly love San Antonio. I'd like to go there with you, Murphy. Have you been there before?"

"No."

"You'll love it. Tell me about the new wing on the hospital."

"A unique concept. A playground indoors, a see-through ceiling so the kids won't feel so confined. Water. A creek bed that runs through it. Sometimes just the sound of rippling water is soothing."

"Wonderful. Your idea?"

"It's not that big a deal."

"To all those kids, it is. And to me because you could think of it. You're a good, good man Murphy. It must be exciting to be able to move around freely."

"I wouldn't call it freedom. More like a prison sometimes. But it's my way."

Not anymore, she thought fiercely and at the same time wished for a giant peanut butter sandwich, thick with jelly. And an ice-cold glass of milk. Convincing Murphy that his life was with her from now on might be a job, but she could handle it. Out of here, she could handle anything.

"What the hell do you mean you found her car in a ditch, but she's nowhere in sight?" Roxanne gripped the phone until her knuckles went white. New fear sent nausea spiraling through her stomach. Danny kept his head close to the receiver so he could listen at the same time.

"Just half an hour ago." The voice on the other end of the line grew louder. "Didn't look like a high-speed crash or anything. Just plopped right into the ditch. The men keep checking the cottage but she isn't there. There are some strange things going on here, though."

Exasperated, Roxanne blew out her breath. "Well? What? Tell me, damn it."

"Inside the cottage, blood . . . only a little. Place is a mess. Mud on the floor. And there was those three guys we caught tooling around in here in their truck. Claimed they were just looking around but we run 'em out anyway." If only he could remember where he'd seen that one man before. . . .

Roxanne's foot tapped out an impatient dance on the floor of the cruise ship. "She might have hit her head when the car left the road. Have you searched all around?"

"Yep. Nobody's seen nothin'. But the gate was crashed through last night. Could have been those guys in that rattletrap truck."

"Crashed gate?" Roxanne took the time to compose herself, resting the receiver on her knee. Her husband gave her shoulders a quick hug.

"Can't be at the entrance twenty-four hours a day, you know. I wouldn't worry about your sister just yet. She could have called someone. They could have taken her somewhere else."

"Listen. I have been calling for hours. She hasn't been home in a long while and she doesn't know anyone around there to call. Get your men out there and comb the place. I'll call back in one hour. You'd better have some answers for me."

Slamming the phone down, Roxanne fought back tears of frustration. "I don't believe this. And I'm hundreds of miles away."

Her handsome husband folded her into his arms. "Everything will be fine. From what I know about your sister, she can take care of herself."

"I should get back there." Roxanne's voice was muffled as she spoke into his shirt. It felt so good to have his arms around her, to hear his reassurance. And he was right. Mackensie could handle herself . . . but if she's hurt and got to wandering around in the woods . . . oh, she couldn't think about that. She'd go crazy. Roxanne paced back and forth as her husband watched helplessly. Something was happening to her sister and there was nothing she could do. A flash of days gone by, of years ago . . . Mackensie had always made sure her baby sister was safe. And now where was she when Mackensie needed her? Miles and miles away.

She wouldn't crack. She wouldn't fall apart. But deep down, she felt real fear. Roxanne wrapped her arms around herself and forced herself to stop pacing.

Learning fast about a woman's moods, her husband led her toward the lido deck. A good bout of blackjack could take up to an hour and just might help her get her mind off her dark imaginings. At least it might keep her from holding the captain hostage and forcing him to turn the ship for home. Danny squeezed Roxanne to him. "Call them back in an hour. If there's still no news, we'll call my brother. He can go down and check things out for us."

"Yes," she agreed, pressing her sunburned cheek against his strong arm. "At least he would care more than those guys."

Swamp. Milkweed. Broomsage. God knows what's in here with us. She remembered the brochures. Cane-brake rattlers. Puffing adders. Banded water snakes. Mac prayed. She knew if a snake slithered across her shins she would scream so loud the tourists at the scenic lookout on Morrow Mountain would hear her. Along with the deranged threesome that searched for them. Tall grass grabbed at her ankles. Her footsteps sank into the muddy bog, making the going rough and strength-draining. She swore to herself that when she got out of this she was going to soak in a bubble bath for three days.

Deeper and deeper into the woods they moved. The ground became vertical and difficult to manage. Murphy no longer held her hand but went ahead and held branches or kicked weeks and underbrush out of her way.

She ran into Murphy's back. He had come to an abrupt halt and was staring at something.

Mac peeked around his large frame and followed his gaze. THE ENCHANTED FOREST. A dull and rusting wrought-iron frame swung over an archway proclaiming they'd just reached the threshold of fantasy land? She laughed. It started out as a ridiculous giggle and ended up being a smothered chuckle.

"This is really stupid. Enchanted forest? Hah!"

A row of listing fences twisted in two directions, strangled by the foliage. The ground beyond the sign went steeply up. At least it was away from the swampland they had been trudging through for the last two hours.

Murphy grunted. "I remember something about this place. Haunted." He nodded. "That's why it was deserted years ago."

"This whole part of the forest has a lurking kind of attitude, but haunted? I doubt it." She closed her fingers around Murphy's arm and looked around just the same.

He grinned a weary smile and pulled his arm to him, bringing her up against him. "I didn't say I agree. Let's go."

She looked up. It was going to be a good climb and she was already drooping. She looked down at their hands joined and back to his beautiful eyes and followed him without reservation.

"In combat things move quickly." He explained as he

climbed. "Spontaneously. Decisions are made in seconds that mean life or death. The more I think about this situation, I feel there's only one way out. Right through them. We're probably about two miles from the cottage. We'll get you back there."

She looked back over her shoulder. Dark shadows and light wavered eerily, black and mocking. Churned earth and compost marked their footsteps. Whatever was ahead couldn't be any worse.

His mind thrashed at possibilities. He had to find out where the three men were. He had to get her out of danger. Maybe he'd just kill them for the fun of it. For putting her through this.

"I'm tired and I'm hungry," Turk whined.

Harry's fist shot out before he could duck, and Turk took the full power of it. Reeling back, he swiped at blood trickling from his mouth. "Damn, Harry. You're obsessed with this."

Harry's eyes flashed lightning. "No crummy little flirt makes a fool of me. I get madder every time I think of him sending her in to scope us out. How the hell did he figure any of this out?" He ground his fist into the palm of his other hand.

The other two men looked at each other. They were tired of this. Neither one of them wanted to be anywhere in the Uwharrie Forest. They felt the eeriness and danger even if Harry didn't. And the unspoken worry between them, that Harry had gone around the bend, festered in each mind.

They had hidden the truck and had plunged into the forest hours ago. There were signs of the woman and her friend here and there, but no clear trail. It was beginning to look like an impossible task.

As if he were reading their minds, Harry whirled on

them. "Either one of you thinking about running out on me? Don't. I'll shoot you as easy as one of them. If you two hadn't screwed up the works, we would be on our way somewhere far away."

Sully wearily voiced an option. "Can't we think of some way to flush them out? Set the place on fire!"

Harry snorted. "Sure and bring the whole world down on us. Use your head."

Turk looked back in the direction of the cottage. "Think they'll try to get back there?"

"It's a possibility. Probably going to lay low for a while and then light out for the police. Whatever, we have food and water. They don't. One of you is going to plant your ass near the cottage. The other is going to take the truck and scan the roads, inside and outside of this place. We'll meet back here toward dark."

The two men exchanged another look. They were just afraid enough of Harry to do what he told them to do. Between them they decided who would take which task. Turk volunteered to stake out the cottage. Sully decided to take the truck. He was hoping the activity would soothe his nerves. "How do I drive in and out of here with that guard at the gate?"

"Figure it out. Kill him and hide his body if you need to."

Sully passed on that idea. He might be in for a good robbery but not a killing. He'd drive that damn truck somewhere, get out where he figured they wouldn't be, and after a while he'd go back and confess to not finding them. He wanted this over. He'd sneak back, get some of the money, and split. He'd go so far away Harry would forget his name.

Alone now, Harry allowed his fury and anger to press him on. He'd find them or he'd die trying. He'd fix that girl and make her friend watch. Then he'd blow them both away. They'd never be found. Nothing but a pile of old bleached bones hidden under the moss and sticks of this horrible place. Shaking his head, he pushed on. Determination drove him; sanity slowly slipped away.

Nine

*"Yeah, open up the wounds and bleed to death
in the name of getting well. . . ."*

Vines snaked their way across the ground and up into
the forlorn buildings. Prickly, wide-leafed plants sprouted
from the damp soil to inhabit the settlement. Huge weeds
sporting large, fanning blossoms crept up to twine around
the trunks of the trees. The humidity hung in the air.

Murphy hacked away at the stalks as they moved deep
into the center with him pulling the foliage in behind
them. The biggest challenge was going to be convincing
her to let him get on with it. Alone.

Skeletal remains of homes that were started on hopes
and dreams jutted skyward. Moss clung to the north side
of a house that had simply leaned, fallen halfway, and given
up. They came upon another structure, devoid of window
glass with vines wandering across the floor, but it was dry
and had a roof still intact. They entered the house, testing
the strength of the rotting floorboards as they went. Murphy cut at the vines and tossed them back outside.

Relieved, if only temporarily, Mackensie pulled her
shoes off. Mac dropped beside her beneath the window
and soon she was stretched out perpendicular to him with
her head on his thigh. "Can you think while I'm talking?"

He could. In fact it would help. Reality kept trying to
slip out of reach. His mind wanted to equate his surround-

ings and his situation to the long days and longer nights in Vietnam. She kept him tethered to the ground.

She wiped at some of the dirt clinging to her arms. Again she yearned for a bath. A Jacuzzi. A big one. Champagne glasses on the rim, candles flickering in the dim light, and music, low, lazy romantic sounds. Resting her arm lightly over her eyes, she sighed. "You know, Murphy, I went to New York with my eyes wide open. Hopes. Amazing how we live from one day to the next on dreams. That city seems light-years away."

Dreams were something Thomas Justice Murphy had shrugged off years ago. He liked that she still had them. Whenever he let down his guard, he usually found himself thinking about a lot of other things. The fact that those thugs had literally, physically put a stop to his way of life was another good reason to decide which way he would make them pay.

"I was going to be an actress. It didn't work out, of course. Dreams rarely do. I settled, Murphy. I thought it was okay. But not now. I was going to use my time at Tillery to figure out my next move. My apartment is fashionable. I knew all the, quote, right people. Made the right contacts. We did New York evenings, dinners, plays. And it wasn't enough. I thought staying here a few extra days would change my perspective and determine what I want to do with my life. I don't think I'll ever take anything for granted again. And as for settling, never again. Time is too precious to waste." She reached up and ran her fingers across his lips. He kissed her hand. She loved the feel of him. "Do you believe in destiny, Murphy?"

The sound of her voice pleased him, transported him. "I haven't thought much about it." The hell he hadn't, his brain objected. "Why?"

"Well, you've got to admit, not many other people have met this way. It was just meant to be, Murphy." When he didn't respond, she twisted so she could look up at him. "Don't you think our paths were meant to cross?"

And probably split again. The thought unsettled him.

He was whittling the end of a sapling branch to a fine point with his knife. Testing it with his finger, he pretended to be distracted by his project. The last thing he wanted was to disappoint her. If he were a different sort of man, he wouldn't. But he wasn't, and remembering all too well that things often happen that are out of control, he didn't want to commit. Not until he was sure he knew what it meant.

He answered idly and matter-of-factly. "I believe the man upstairs has a plan for us but it's up to us to work our way there." He blew scrapings off the stick and smoothed it with his finger. Was she the type that wanted promises? Yes, he figured she was. He could never make any. He went back to the work on his project, all the while his mind plotting and scheming.

She studied the gash that crossed the back of her hand. It was almost comforting that he felt that way. "That could be. What part do you think this plays in all of it?"

He shrugged and smiled at her. "I don't know. Who really knows or ever finds out what part leads to the other part? You don't have time to think—sometimes the fork in the road looms up and you have to make a move. On occasion I've tried to figure out what part Vietnam played in all this. In Nam time was accelerated. I was afraid it would move too slowly back here for me. Sometimes it does."

"It does? That scares me."

"It shouldn't scare you. At first it was freeze-framed. So much had changed. And too much had stayed the same. No one wanted to know that you served in Vietnam. No one wanted to hear what you had to say. Soon the pride you felt in doing a job you were sent to do, by those very same people, withers from keeping it inside."

"Pride. I'm proud of you and every other man or woman who served this country. And I understand all of what you say, Murphy, but it was such a long time ago."

He put his arm around her and pulled her close to him. "Once you've lived like that, it's part of you. A shadow that's plastered against your soul. And as far as your understanding it, I don't think so. You can't."

"Okay. I can accept that. But now there's sunshine and rain, beaches and mountains, cool summer evenings and snug snowy nights in front of a fireplace to look to. And there's me. There's me now, Murphy. Maybe it'll take the edge off."

Resting his head back against the wall, he wondered. "I'm not going to change. I've been the same man all my life, just in different stages."

"That's good enough for me. I think you're something very special just the way you are." She reached up and ran her fingers across his beard-roughened jaw. He was genuine. He was part of her now and that's another thing that wouldn't change. "You're like," she shook her head trying to think of the right words, "like a jewel. One cut with a few facets is beautiful. One that is multifaceted is intricate, complex, and perpetually fascinating. You're like that treasure and I'll never tire of looking into the angles, whether they flash light or shadows." She reared up to plant a small kiss on his lips. "Ever hear of PTSD, Murphy?"

"Sure. Post traumatic stress disorder."

"I feel pretty certain that you've got it." She held her breath, hoping he didn't take her the wrong way. But she needed to make him think about it. For them. For him.

He snorted. "You didn't tell me you had your degree in psychiatry."

"You don't sound surprised."

"That's because I've heard it before. I just don't believe it."

She put her hand on his wrist to stop that damned whittling. He set the stick and the knife down and brushed at her hair with one hand, the other cupping her head. "Why not? It's certainly not something to be ashamed of." Her brother had been and she had never been able to handle that.

"I've been out of Nam for years. And if I had it, I surely wouldn't be ashamed of it. Shame is not one of my feelings associated with Nam. I was a soldier. To us it was kill or be killed. That simple."

"The fact that Nam was a long time ago has nothing to do with it. Think back to the minute guns started firing when the cops were chasing you. Can you tell me that didn't trigger memories and a very strong will not to get nailed?"

"It did. That's called protecting yourself." He had admitted to himself already that lots of things jettisoned him back there lately. But it was just the circumstances. Nothing else.

"Murphy, when you broke into the cottage, you were like a hunted wolf. You were willing to tear flesh from bones in order to live. It makes sense. For a while you were working beyond the range of human emotion. The more I watched you, the more you reminded me of someone else. Someone who let PTSD kill him. My brother." She sat up and rested her back against the wall next to him.

The heavy sadness pained her chest as always when she let herself remember. "The family suffered nearly as much. He couldn't hold a job. His nightmares kept him from resting. He took serious offense to comments about the vets. If anybody ticked him off, he tore into them. He drank a lot. One night, in a bar outside of town, someone made a crack about the jacket he wore, the one with his company patch and 'Vietnam Veteran and Proud of It' plastered across the back." She drew her knees up and encircled them with her arms.

"The police came by to tell us he was in City Hospital.

I'll never forget the look on my parents' faces. They didn't want me to go, but I did. He was cut up bad. I'll never forget him lying in that bed. Every damn thing was white, blaring white. I finally got some time alone with him. The folks went down for coffee. He held my hand. I said 'Don't talk, Austin. Rest. You need to get strong again.' " Remembering always hurt so badly. Tears pushed their way to the surface.

Murphy put his arm around her shoulders and pulled her snug against him.

"He grinned up at me and said, 'Mac, where I'm going there's plenty of rest. I don't want you to be sad. It don't mean nothin'. It was over a long time ago. Don't cry, baby. I want to remember you smiling at me.' I dried my tears and I smiled for him. He kissed me and he died. Damn him, he died right under my hands. If it had been recognized as PTSD, if someone had been able to help him, he would be alive and happy today. I've seen the symptoms. You handle it all very well. You have a stronger mind, a better handle on restraint, but I still think you have it."

"Don't worry about me. I'm fine. I've been taking care of myself for a long time now."

"I can't help but worry. The only reason someone wants to take care of someone else is because of love. The love of a family member, a real, true once-in-a-lifetime friend or a lover. Why would anyone else care? I want to see you happy. Completely happy."

He drew her tighter against him. He felt the power of her actually tremble through his body. No one had ever moved him so.

She snuggled next to him and reveled in the feeling. She'd have to think of ways to show him, to prove to him that her feelings were deep and genuine and not inclined in the least to change.

"I'll be back." She moved to get up.

He grabbed her arm and plopped her back on the floor beside him. "Don't go wandering around out there."

"I won't," she assured him. "I'll stay close. Before you can count to sixty, I'll be back."

He watched her scoot back out the door and found himself counting, one, two, three, four . . . damn it, he didn't have time for this. He had to plan his strategy. He had to map a tactic.

Fifty-eight, fifty . . . Delayed stress syndrome. Hah!

She was back and standing before him like a twelve-year-old with a secret. A strong rush of pleasure washed over him. Dirt streaked her face and arms. Her hands were behind her back.

God, she loved looking at him. Seeing him battered and beat up, she imagined what he looked like in combat. Not so very different, she suspected. Carefully, so as not to break the fragile stems, she brought both hands in front. They were filled to overflowing with delicate violet flowers. She slowly knelt down before him and, presenting them to him, put them across his lap. Then, picking up one of the small blooms, she passed it over her lips, leaned forward to gently draw the tiny petals of the flower across his mouth. Leaning forward, she followed the motion with a kiss. One so gentle, so dainty and sweet that he found himself leaning toward her as if in a trance.

His heart jerked painfully in his chest. Not one person in his entire life had reached in, grabbed hold of his heart, and pulled so hard. But this woman, this woman-child, who looked at him with such love in her warm green eyes set him back. Without realizing it, he untied some of the knots in his heart, uncurled some of the ropes around his soul. Not all the way. Part of him would always be just that, personal. His and no one else's, but the biggest part was freeing up. He didn't know whether to choke her or kiss her.

He brought one finger at a time against his mouth and pressed his lips to them, adoring her. Her wrist where the pulse skipped double-time. Inside her elbow where a mere touch of his mouth drew a quiet moan from her lips.

She fell into his arms and crushed his mouth beneath hers. She wanted to feel it again, the mindless pitch of emotions, to join and forge into his very being. His work-roughened hands were at once gentle and frenzied as they roved over her body, kindling fiery sensations.

It felt good, and so very right. That part of him that had been off axis for years righted itself. She was crushing the flimsy blooms between them and releasing the sweet, rich aroma, which rose to mix and mingle with the hot ferocity of hunger and passion.

He worked the remaining buttons on her shirt loose and slipped his hand inside. She fit to him. Like she was fashioned and set upon this earth to please him and to be pleased by him.

His body responded beneath hers and she celebrated in the power of it. A tall, strong man moved, stirred by her hands, her mouth. And the way he could render her his, by the mere look in his eyes, quiver of his muscles, strength of his embrace, astonished her.

Rolling, spilling the flowers to the floor, she locked one leg around his and hung on. Pressed against the full length of him, she felt nothing could ever threaten her again. She was safe and protected and cherished. She never again wanted to be without what he brought to her. Together, together, they could love the whole stupid world away.

His mouth roamed her face, her throat, and found the bared flesh of her shoulders. She brought his mouth back to hers and whispered against them, "Love me, Murphy, love me."

She felt the sudden tension in his body before she heard it. Just the snap of a twig. Only the slightest movement of air. Someone was approaching. Quietly. Steadily. And they were getting close.

Murphy's hand came down to cover her mouth ever so lightly.

His voice was low as he slowly spelled out the plan that was being forced on him. That split second-decision instinct again. "It could be one or all of them. When the mess starts, take off out of here. Work your way up from here and around to the south. Follow the road but keep to the trees. Get to the cottage and call the law." When she started to object, he leaned over and silenced her with a kiss. "Trust me. I can take care of myself but I have to know you're far away from here."

Alone? Covering the terrain by herself was a terrifying thought. She was scared. More so now than on the first night. Terrified for him. She wouldn't let him see it.

Desperation betrayed itself in her voice. "When this is over, you won't run out on me?"

He took a fleeting moment to feast his eyes on her. His hand moved gently to her hair and then came down to frame her face. "When this is over, I'll buy you a big fat steak in an atmospheric candlelit restaurant and we'll dance until dawn."

Her heart was pounding. Thoughts swam in her head. A picture of them formed in her mind. She would wear a fine silk dress, one that flowed with each movement. Sapphire blue, shadowed dark and then light as she swayed in his arms. Diamonds at her ears and her hair piled high on her head and clipped with a clasp that would easily pull free so that later he could release it and watch her hair flow over her shoulders. He would be clean and rested and dressed in a dark gray suit, western cut. He'd smell of spicy after-shave and he would lead her to the dance floor, her fingertips held gently in his. She would whirl into the circle of his arms and they would join each other in a world made just for them by romantic music and wavering, soft lights. People would look at them and sigh. They would be beautiful together.

She crouched down beside him and watched as he peered out the paneless window, gauging and planning. Her first thought was the uneasiness about his safety, but the reflection soon dissolved when she saw the look in his eyes. Still, she didn't want to leave him. She could only do this for him. For herself she would have chosen to stay, but for him, she must leave.

All the survival instincts he'd lived with for so long began their run through his brain. He was aware that she was plastering herself against his back, hugging him for all she was worth. But his eyes, his mind were on that lone figure making its way closer and closer, brandishing a weapon in front of him. He had to take this man down before he could warn the others. For a moment he was back in Nam, face blackened, crouched position, his weapon poised and ready. He could smell the man. Stiletto and spear at the ready, he gauged it to be twenty seconds before his move. He felt her desperation, her reluctance.

How could he ever tell her how much she meant to him? That he loved her like nothing and no one else in his life. The words might come out wrong.

The blood coursed through her veins. There was so much she wanted to say to him. So much she wanted him to know. There was no time now. Bravely, she squared her shoulders. "Murphy. See you later."

The second he felt her release him, he turned and grabbed her by the front of her shirt, scooped up a handful of spilled blossoms from the floor and shoved them in her hand. "Later, lady." He crushed her mouth beneath his and then pushed her away, his eyes clouded with a fierceness that frightened her even more. "Go. Now."

Purposefully, he whirled for the doorway and she ran through the back. She heard him charge, heard the surprised exclamation, scuffling and muttered curses. Mackensie heard the smart crack of a breaking bone. She sucked in her breath and ran. She ran for her life. For his life. For theirs.

Sully had been ready to turn back, satisfied to report to Harry that he'd seen no one, when a monster who came at him feet first, one booted foot shattering his left knee-cap. He fell to the ground.

She ran for all she was worth, limbs smacking at her face and tearing deep scratches across her arms. The sound of splintering bone followed her, echoing in her mind.

Sully clenched both hands around his ruined knee and groveled. Murphy picked up the rifle and slung the strap over his shoulder. Looking down at the man, he wondered if Mackensie might just be right about PTSD. He surely felt no remorse.

"Where's the rest of your gang?"

Sully wailed and rolled his head back and forth. Pain as he'd never known before sliced through his entire body. He waited and nearly welcomed the bullet he figured he was going to get. "Don't know, man. Christ, just kill me and get it over with."

"Kill you, hell. You'll limp the rest of your life from cell block to mess hall, yard and back. And you'll remember. Now, where are your buddies?"

Sully moaned, loudly, and then slipped into the relief of darkness.

Eventually, the forest around her grew silent except for the occasional startled flight of a bird or scurry of an animal. She figured the storm must finally be moving in. Pausing to catch her breath, she leaned against the old bumpy bark of a tree and looked skyward. *Please, God, protect him. I want him in my life for a long, long time.*

* * *

Murphy looked down at the man who had lost consciousness. The cold, hard steel of the weapon he'd relieved him of felt good. One down and two to go. Mackensie should be close to reaching the cottage. She would get the law and this could move from beginning to end, right now.

It was late afternoon. Mackensie kept out of sight. Thirst wrestled with her throat. Her heart threatened to burst right inside her rib cage from the exertion. Her legs ached and her scratched arms stung.

It couldn't be much farther.

The curves of the road were becoming familiar. Going on, she felt the rush of tears to her eyes. It was there! She could see the roof. Her walk became a jog, then a sprint, and finally she broke into a run.

Plowing through the last stand of trees, not even thinking of anything except that the end to all this was nearly here, Mackensie ran across the porch and slammed open the front door.

The man whirled from his walk from kitchen to living room couch, nearly as startled as she.

It couldn't be, her mind screamed. She forced her body into gear and turned around and ran.

Turk dropped his plate on the floor and dashed after her. Harry would kill him if he let her get away now. Diving for her, he grabbed her around the waist and sent both of them tumbling down the slight incline.

"No!" she screamed. Fighting, kicking, biting, Mackensie tried to get away. Blood pounded in her ears; desperation forced her mind to keep working. She heard the man's muffled curses at the same time she saw him draw back a fist. She was sinking deeper and deeper into a bottomless pit. Murphy. Her last conscious thought was of him.

She heard laughter. Somewhere far away someone was knee-slapping happy. And then the dark slowly faded to light and she remembered.

Harry and Turk sat across from each other at the breakfast bar, each holding a can of beer. The cottage was trashed. Through half-closed eyes, Mackensie could see the remnants of paper plates on the floor amid a mountain of empty beer cans.

She had blundered right into the midst of them. Her first rational thought was that there was danger of Murphy walking in on all this, as innocent as she.

No, he was smarter than that. But she had to make sure it didn't happen. Despite her will, the safe darkness of unconsciousness toyed with her.

"Look, Turk, the lady's awake. Well now, sweet thing." Harry strolled to the couch and knelt down, lifted a lock of her hair, held it in his hand, and tugged. "What do you have to say to good ole Harry?"

That voice. It jerked her back to reality, swiftly. *Sit on a hand grenade* was the first thing to come to her mind. But then the old stand-by cliché popped out of her mouth in a threatening tone of voice she didn't recognize as her own. "You won't get away with this."

Harry laughed. He threw his head back, slapped his hands on his thighs, and roared. His laughter was good for her. It fired her anger and sent her fear scurrying for cover.

"Hear that, Turk, my friend. We won't get away with this." He pushed his face close to hers. "Oh, yes we will. And not you or your boyfriend will be around to do anything about it."

Turk felt the hair rise at the back of his neck. No killing. That's what Harry had promised them at the beginning. But it was all changing. Everything had gone wrong. He was getting more and more scared by the minute.

Harry's dirty fingers played with the collar of her shirt, slipping underneath to tease the skin at her throat. "Where's lover boy?"

She rolled her head away from his touch as he ran his fingers over her cheek where an ugly bruise was forming.

"As soon as Sully shows up," he told Turk, smugly, "we're going to take the little miss here for a walk. One way or another you have to die. Wouldn't you rather do it in his arms? You shouldn't have double-crossed me. I would 'a treated you right." His hand brushed over her breast and squeezed.

Outraged, Mackensie rolled to a sitting position and kicked her legs out, striking him on the shin. She was rewarded by him putting both his hands on her shoulders as he pushed her back. Straddling her lap, his knees on the couch cushions, he brought his mouth dangerously close to hers.

"Don't hurry things, darlin'. Before I kill you I'm going to learn what you have that a man will risk his life for. And I'm going to make him watch. Yep. Watch it all."

Turk's blood turned to ice water. He couldn't stop Harry once he got going. Turk wanted out of this.

Turk knew only one way to get Harry's mind off the girl's body and her betrayal. The money. He moved to the bedroom and rushed back carrying a battered satchel.

Harry's weight was oppressive. His intentions were clear. It was all she could do to keep from screaming when he unbuttoned the next button on her shirt. He ran his rough hand over the smooth curve of her breast.

He didn't like it that she didn't look away in disgust, or beg for mercy. But he knew that when he had the boyfriend tied to a chair and spread her out on the floor in front of him . . . it would be a different story. He leaned forward, holding her head between both his hamlike hands and crushing his mouth on hers.

She reacted instinctively. Her hands might be tied behind her back, but she still had shoulders and knees and she reciprocated with both. A sharp jerk of her knees connected with him and he rolled off her. He couldn't stand straight but that didn't stop him from drawing his hand back. She didn't flinch.

"No, I won't hit you. Your time is coming. I'll make you pay, slowly. Both of you."

Turk had never treated a woman as Harry was using this girl. Christ, he had a mother and six sisters. "Harry. Look. Let's take this money and run. We don't have to go back for the rest. We'll have a good head start and be long gone. We could even go to Mexico." He smiled, happy with his impromptu idea.

Harry was across the room in a split second to backhand Turk across the face. Turk staggered backward, hurt and confusion playing across his face. He clutched the bag to his chest. "Fool. Sully has the damn truck. Besides, that man out there won't let this rest, you can be sure of that."

Where was he? He had to be out there somewhere. Or on his way here.

"Okay, okay, Mrs. Pike. We'll call in the law. That old beat-up truck I told you about was still parked alongside the road. I still can't figure out what they want here. They might just know something about your sister's whereabouts all right. I'm worried myself now."

"You're darn right you'll call in the law. And I expect you and the other security men to be scouring the woods. Go back to the cottage and check it out again. I don't care if you were just there a couple of hours ago. Find my sister. And find her now. I'll check back in an hour."

"Better give us at least two hours. Don't know where I'll be."

Roxanne slammed the phone down and turned to her patient husband. "Something's happened to her. Or maybe right this very minute she's being hurt by that bunch in the pickup."

Danny patted her head and shushed her. He wouldn't for the world let her know how worried he was. She needed him to be strong, but the whole thing sounded really bad to him. Three mug-uglies on the loose and her pretty sister, alone and lost. "I'll go ahead and call my brother."

"I want to call my parents, but they're hours away. Oh, Lord, I can't stand much more of this."

Jeb turned to the other security officers. "I'm calling in the law. It could be that they're the three guys who robbed the auto parts store in Concord a couple of days ago. They're on the run, you know. One of you go back to the cottage. The others get in your trucks and patrol. Anything out of the ordinary, report it."

The men didn't have to be told twice. Most of them had seen the derelicts in the truck. A beautiful woman would be a feast to those creeps. This was getting personal.

Murphy crouched down in the bushes close to the house. The lights were on. There was no sign of the law. They had to be in there with her. Both of them. He knew where the third man was and knew for certain that he wouldn't be moving around for a long while.

Making his way soundlessly around to the side window, he made a move upward to look in. At that moment the security patrol drove right up the road and screeched to a halt in front of the cottage. They would march right up and knock on the door. He needed them out of here. He jumped back into the bushes and waited.

There was only one man. Murphy watched him climb out of the truck and begin his walk toward the cottage.

"Quiet. Get over here." He motioned for the security man to join him in the shadows.

The guard froze.

Christ, Murphy realized the guard thought he was one of the criminals. "Over here, you damn fool. They've probably got a girl held hostage in there."

Motionless, the guard stood still as any statue. The curtain at the window began to move. Murphy made a dive for the security man, flattened him with a slamming right hook, and dragged him across the ground into the shrubbery.

The uniformed officer began to fight him and Murphy drew back a solid fist, putting him out of his turmoil. Too much was at stake to be polite.

Murphy knew they would see the patrol vehicle and be on guard. It would be enough to draw their attention to the front so that Murphy could get in there before they could hurt her. He headed around to the back of the cottage.

Ten

*"You blamed us and you shamed us,
but, by God, you never tamed us. . . ."*

"It's the security guys." Turk peeked through the curtains of the front window. His hand began to shake and he resolutely forced it to stop. He turned to Harry for a lead on the next move. He silently cursed his own stupidity at letting himself get pulled into this. Too damn late now.

Harry was glad. He was elated. Things were coming to a head. If security was here, then *he* couldn't be far behind. It was time. Time for the man who screwed up their plans to suffer. And suffer he would. The mental pain he would hand that man as he took and took his woman right under his nose would cripple him. Harry laughed and Mackensie heard the insanity in the sound.

Harry got serious, fast. "Security, huh? They've been enough of a pain in the butt. Let the big dudes come on." He grabbed a handful of Mackensie's hair and dragged her along to the window with him. Roughly jamming Turk aside, he stood in front of the window. Knocking the curtains aside, he peered out. He couldn't see anything except the patrol vehicle parked up along the road. Where were the cowards? Where the hell was Sully?

"Your boyfriend a little late getting here? That's okay. It gives me time to get to know you better." He mashed her mouth beneath his and ran a hand over her breast.

She shoved at him and wiped her mouth with the back of her hand, but she stopped short of spitting on the floor.

Armed now with the gun taken from the thug in the Enchanted Forest, Murphy ran up the few steps that led from the side hill and made his way to the north window. One wrong move, one mistimed action and his plan could backfire. He could get her killed. In Nam it had been simply him and his ability to keep himself and his men alive. Here, today, in the good old US of A, it was the same. His brain kicked into overdrive. His heart steeled itself for whatever happened.

Reaching the window, he came up slowly under it. Only seconds had ticked by since he'd downed the security man and made his way to the back. Murphy watched as Harry ran his hands over Mackensie. Something undefinable streaked through him. She hadn't deserved this. Any of it. He watched her fight, her humiliation hidden beneath defiance. It was now or never.

Just the fact that he hesitated worried him. It was because of Mackensie, he admitted to himself, and wished she hadn't come to mean life itself to him.

He didn't want bullets flying unless it was absolutely the only choice. He shifted over to the back door, braced himself, let his brain click into full-kill mode, and charged the door.

Wood trembled, splintered, and cracked, giving way to the solid wave of warrior coming through. He saw all three bodies turn in unison. As if frozen, the three of them stopped, paralyzed. Mackensie's eyes flew wide open. What she saw coming toward them had ferocious eyes, a vicious mouth, and a savage growl coming from his throat. She tensed, waiting for the explosion. She had never seen such malevolence. It sent frigid fear skittering through her. These men were going to be torn to pieces.

Harry had Mackensie by the hair and swung her in front of him for a shield. She ducked and spun, attempting to knock him off balance. The bullet he fired hit the ceiling, sending splinters flying.

Turk was the first threat, gun nervously waggling in the air in front of him, the look of a surprised devil on his face. Murphy lunged at him and at the same time brought his foot across Harry's kneecaps, buckling him to the floor and dragging Mackensie with him.

Sliding, with Turk caught under Murphy's fist, they crashed against the wall. Before Harry could make a move to get up, Murphy threw a karate punch at his face, holding him down a second longer. Smashing a fist into Turk's face brought instant satisfaction as Murphy watched the man dive into near unconsciousness.

Mackensie tried to roll away, but Harry still had a tight hold on her hair. Gaining his feet, he hauled her up with him. And then she felt the dreaded ice-cold weight of steel, resting an inch to the left of her temple. If Murphy didn't see it, didn't sum up the situation in one infinitesimal second, the gun would go off . . . and it would be all over. She mustered all her strength and twisted, throwing her elbow into Harry. It only served to make him stronger and he jerked her by the handful of hair and pushed her up against the wall, trapping her there with his body.

Rolling, coming up under Harry, Murphy jabbed the end of the gun upward under his chin. And then he saw. Harry's finger was on the trigger of a gun that was plastered against Mackensie's head. He stopped dead, gun gripped tightly in his hand.

Harry laughed, an overconfident giggle with a large dose of nervousness underneath. "Gotcha, lover boy. Back off or I squeeze this trigger and splatter the pretty girl's brains all over you." He became serious fast. "I'd love that, lover boy, so you just push me."

Keeping his gun on Harry, Murphy slowly backed away. Chances were he could take him out. But did he dare risk it? Pure reaction could have Harry's fingers closing on the trigger, tripping the hammer, and . . .

Harry pulled Mackensie square in front of him. Reading Murphy's mind, he leered. "Don't try it." He glowered at Murphy and, keeping his eyes on the man and the gun at Mackensie's head, let his lips graze her shoulder, reveling in the flash of reaction that knifed through Murphy's eyes.

It was then he decided death was too good for Harry. Murphy planted his feet firmly apart and waited. To guess Harry's next move could hurry death.

"If you'd just run, none of this would have happened. Your girlfriend here wouldn't have to die." Turk moaned and Harry tightened up, never taking his eyes off Murphy. "Get up, Turk."

Turk stood, still woozy. Sizing up the situation, he made a move for his gun and realized that Murphy had the toe of one boot, trapping it to the floor beside him. Turk felt weak and queasy. All he wanted to do was run, but he knew lead would rip through his back and drain him dry. Hardly breathing, he remained, fighting the nausea that threatened to embarrass him.

"Put the gun down, cowboy." Harry's steely eyes challenged Murphy. "Put it down or I'll simply break her neck right now."

Giving up the weapon would be the wrong move. If anyone else had been between him and the perpetrator, there would be no question. No second thoughts, he'd pull the trigger and take his chances, but it was Mackensie. She stood bravely, chin jutting upward, lips pressed together in resignation. Seconds ticked by.

The two men eyed each other like two mongrel dogs before a fight. Blood would be shed this night, Mackensie thought. And no way was it going to be Murphy's. Only a span of three quick minutes had passed since Murphy had burst in through the back door. But in the instant it took to pull a breath, it was about to be over. Mackensie curled her fingers into a fist and turned her knuckles back toward Harry.

Thomas Justice Murphy watched Harry and waited for the blink, the tick, the one variance that would alert him to Harry making his next move.

It was Mackensie who sensed it first. Only the slightest twitch of muscle, but she took the chance. Bringing her clenched fingers up and using a full-arm swing, she brought her fist down, swift and punishing and hard on the mark. Right between Harry's legs.

Gut-wrenching pain shot straight up through him. A roar trembled from his lips as fury brought him strength. Winded and shocked, Harry howled. Unable to keep his grasp on the gun, he fumbled it. As he bent over to scoop it up, his other arm fought to keep this wild, fist-flying girl in front of him. He knew, instinctively, if he dropped her, he'd be a clear target. And he'd die. He crouched against the wall maintaining a death grip on the girl.

All the turmoil had Turk confused. He had to get his gun. Harry would kill him if they got away. He lurched forward. Murphy instinctively turned his gun on him and fired. Turk dropped to the floor, both hands wrapped around a bloody knee.

Mac tried to wrench herself free of Harry's grasp and roll away. Harry's grip was still one of steel. Mackensie looked up. And up. Towering over them was Murphy. The barrel of the gun, pointing inches away from Harry's body, Murphy transfixed for seconds . . . caught between pulling the trigger and not. The fool still held the gun close to her head.

Mackensie waited. Sharp, lethal seconds ticked between them. Mackensie saw the death watch in Murphy's eyes. If he wanted it to happen, willed it, it would be done. She dropped her gaze to the finger that hooked around the trigger. It was still, so very still. But tight, and in intimate contact with the steel.

Her throat went dry.

Harry's head cleared when he looked down the barrel and past it to Murphy's eyes. Shoving himself slowly up the wall, he drew a deep breath. He was going to die. And he'd take the bitch with him.

Murphy took one step closer, lowering the gun from Harry's head. Harry almost sighed in relief. *He's going to back off!* Then Murphy pointed the gun at Harry's heart and sneered, "Let the lady go." Pure, unadulterated terror slammed into Harry's brain. *I'm going to die. Right now. Without a chance to make this man suffer as I had planned. Without a chance to see it all come true.* All he'd worked for up until now. He had nothing to lose now and that made him even more dangerous. But he was scared. Terrified.

Harry did his best to cover it. Hardly able to breathe, he snapped back, "Right. You think I'm stupid."

Turk screamed and writhed in pain. Harry didn't blink an eye. "Shut up, you idiot. Back off, or I'll kill her right now." The arm that was around Mackensie's throat caressed her shoulder.

Dying's too good for him, Murphy resolved. "You asked for this. You and your sidekicks. You're going to remember me. For a long, long time."

Mackensie shuddered. She wanted to press her eyes shut so she didn't have to watch what was going to happen. What she was certain was already moving into action.

Murphy saw the variance he was waiting for. He squeezed the trigger, shattering Harry's knee. Diving for them, Murphy pulled Mackensie free of him and knocked the gun from Harry's hand. They stood a scant twelve inches from each other. Harry's eyes were wide with pain and shock. He slowly slid down the wall to land in a heap at Mac's feet.

"Sweet Jesus," Harry screamed. Holding his bloody knee, he thrashed on the floor beside Turk.

Mackensie held on to Murphy for dear life. Burying her

face in his shirt, she fought the tears that had threatened for so long. She was proud of him. Glad he didn't kill them. For their sake. For Murphy and Mackensie. For the sake of the life she was certain they would have together.

He kissed the top of her head. "Call the law. Wrap a towel around the wounds. I wouldn't want them to bleed to death after I went to great lengths to keep them alive."

Legs wobbly and heart racing, she darted for the phone and called for help. After grabbing towels from the bathroom, she knelt down and wrapped each man's leg. The satisfaction she felt in watching them wallow around in their own blood scared her. But they would have killed her and worse. And then they would have tried to kill the man she loved. Let them bleed.

Sirens blared in the distance. Murphy, keeping his gun on both men, sat back in the chair, exhausted.

"Where's the other man?" Mackensie asked, her trembling easing a bit.

"Nursing a broken leg and tied to the porch."

She knelt beside his chair and put her hands on his arm. "It's over now, Murphy." Mackensie stretched up and pressed her lips to his jaw.

He smiled down at her. "Which restaurant do you want to go to?"

Her laugh was weak. "You did promise me a romantic dinner."

He shook his head. "I don't make promises, kid, but I did say we'd go. And we will."

The sirens were just outside, and before any of them knew what was happening, cops were everywhere. They came in the back way, busting through a side window, and the front door was kicked down. Guns drawn, they assessed the situation quickly. Mackensie thought, for one moment, when the police officer put his hand out for Murphy's gun that Murphy might do something aggressive. She ran her hand down his forearm. "It's really over. Relax. I want to get out of here."

He let the officer have the weapon. Ambulance crews carted off the intruders. An officer had Mackensie in the kitchen, firing questions at her. Murphy sat patiently, puffing on a cigarette, answering yet another officer's questions.

From time to time, Murphy and Mackensie would exchange a glance. She could almost feel his need for a bath and warm food. For rest. Complete, uninterrupted relaxation.

Then and there she vowed to see to his comfort for the rest of her life. But then she almost laughed. Thomas Justice Murphy would have no one see to his comfort but himself.

The questioning over, the directions completed to come to the police department in the morning and sign papers, they were suddenly alone. Closing the door behind the last police officer, Mackensie leaned her back against it, and only because she couldn't stand on her own any longer, she slid silently to sit on the floor. Drawing her knees up, crossing her arms over them, she rested her head. Now that her face was hidden, she let the tears fall. And the cold, stark realization of how close they came to dying, how close she came to losing the chance to be happy with this man, washed through her.

He watched her. It was one of the hardest things he had to do in his life, watch her suffering from what he had brought into her life. He gave her the moment. Let her be for as long as he could. And then he walked toward her, an unspoken vow on his lips. His heart heavy with love . . . and regret. Reaching down, he ever so gently took her hand in his.

Her head flew up and she looked at him through the tears. It sliced through him, scarring him forever. He pulled her to her feet and into the safety of his arms.

They stood in the middle of the destroyed living room and held each other. Arms around each other, his jaw resting at her temple, they embraced. He felt so good beneath her fingers. He cupped the back of her head in his hand, smoothing her hair, pulling her even closer to him.

The clock on the wall behind them registered the passing of time. Yet no time slipped by. They existed only because the other remained. For just a little while there was nothing else but the warm, secure feeling of the other.

A man stood in the doorway and cleared his throat. When they both reluctantly turned to look at him, they recognized the security guard.

"I'll get a crew in here to clean this up. We've been in contact with your sister. She's been calling for hours looking for you. We filled her in. And," he hesitated for a minute, "we hope that you don't blame us."

Mackensie stubbornly wiped at the tears that streaked her face. "We don't blame you for anything." *Get on out of here,* Mac thought. *Leave us alone. Leave us alone.* Then she left Murphy's embrace.

He felt barren, empty. She walked to the door and shut it firmly. He sat back down.

Turning slowly, Mackensie leaned her back against the door and just looked at him. Pleasure feathered its way from her stomach to her heart. Feeling her strength and defiance returning, she smiled at him. She wouldn't feel completely relieved until she got him to the hospital and filled with antibiotics, but the alleviation was there, around the edges.

Moving back to his chair, she merely leaned over and placed a soft kiss on his mouth and proceeded toward the back of the cottage.

"Where are you going?"

She whirled in the hallway and faced him squarely. "Do us both one favor and don't ever ask me that question again."

They laughed. Tired, weak laughter that only promised of happier times to come.

"But I will tell you this time. I'm going to pack a few

things for both of us and then I'm driving you to the hospital." She held up her hand against the protests she knew would follow. "And after that, we're going to find someplace with a huge bathtub and a soft, safe bed."

He grunted his objection but knew better, at this point, than to argue over something that he needed. He knew his fever still existed. He knew his bruised body needed rest, but he'd be the one to decide what action to take. Next time. This time, she needed to direct the action. And he was too damned tired to care at this point.

She waited in the emergency waiting room. Not patiently. What was taking them so long? Two hours passed. It was no surprise to Mackensie to see Murphy stalking out of the emergency room's swinging doors with a nurse at his heels protesting loudly, "But, sir, the doctor wants you kept overnight."

Murphy simply swung back around and faced her. The look he gave her had her turning on her heel and heading back to her business.

Once on the road, Mac sighed and sat back against the seat. "I can't believe it's really over. We can go anywhere, do anything we want to." A large grin covered her face and lit her eyes. "They wanted to keep you, huh?" She was glad he couldn't see her smile in the darkness. "Did they give you a shot of penicillin?"

"Two."

She laughed just because it felt so good and she could picture him dropping his pants.

"Drive," he mumbled.

"Yes, sir. Where do you want to go?"

"We'll go to the auto shop and see if my car is ready. Then we'll find a motel, clean up a little, and find somewhere special to eat. . . ."

He was so sweet. "Murphy, would you mind if we waited

for that special dinner? I mean, I would like to be able to wear a sexy dress and makeup and everything is back at the cottage. Let's just find a pizza place tonight."

He'd give her anything. Now. Just for now.

She drove to the garage. His little convertible sat on the lot. The business was closed for the night. He'd never been glad to see a car before, but then his life was becoming filled with firsts.

She eyed the sporty little car and exclaimed happily, "All right! You didn't say it was a convertible. Let's go."

Murphy left a note for the mechanic on the windshield of the truck. He reached for the extra key to the convertible that was stuck under the wheel well, and climbed in beside her.

She looked over at him and beamed. "Would you put the top down, Murphy?"

He pleased her and then himself as he pulled from the lot, watching her as she scooted up on top of the back of the seat and rode like a queen in a parade down Main Street. Her hair blown back by the wind, her grin wide, and her dirty face aglow. His own smile started deep in his gut to finally reach his lips. But there was sadness near the surface. They'd have their good time. And then he would go. He would let her get on with her life. Without him.

"Go faster, Murphy. Go faster." She let out a rebel yell that turned a few heads as they passed by. Amazed by her energy, he pressed the pedal to the floor.

Finding a diner on the edge of town, they parked and he would have had to run to keep up with her. So he followed. "Cheeseburgers. Ten of them. And fries, greasy and salty and drowned in ketchup." She turned suddenly, planted a kiss smack on his mouth, and then continued to run toward the door of the diner, tugging him along behind. He could live a lifetime on her spontaneity. Leaving her was going to kill him. "And a milk shake. Chocolate." Having just climbed the first step, she turned

suddenly and launched herself into his arms. He caught
her and lowered his mouth to hers. It was like sinking into
heaven. "Oh, Lord, Murphy, we're free."

She ate like a marine and he satisfied his own empty stomach with steak and potatoes and an ice-cold beer or two.

Outside again, she begged, "Let's walk. I want to take
a walk and then we're going to find a motel and . . ." She
lit two cigarettes and handed him one.

He stood in the shadows of the diner's neon light watching this flurry of activity that had him by the hand and
wondered, again, if he was man enough to do what was
right. She really thought she loved him. She truly believed
it. He doubted that he could ever convince her that it was
just a result of a lot of outside things. The situation they
were in, the forces of having to fight for their lives together . . . bull. He was in love with her. In heart-stopping
love for the first time in his life. But it was too late. He
couldn't change the man he was.

They strolled hand in hand around the block and back
to the car. He had never been on the receiving end of such
devotion. But it couldn't last. She would find some other
lucky man to be the recipient of all she had to give so freely.
She settled into an easy silence as they strolled, and he realized how exhausted she was. He guided her back toward
the diner.

Back at the car, she jumped in the driver's side. "I'll
drive this time. Tell me where to go."

He didn't object when she screeched out of the parking
lot. The newfound independence was finally seeping into
him also. And it felt so damn good. Just watching her,
being near her was the best thing that had ever happened
to him. Getting used to life without her was going to be
hell. But then he'd been there before, too.

"Turn right."

"Then?"

"About two miles away is an inn I worked on some years

back. It has fireplaces in every room and a bathroom as big as a bedroom with whirlpool baths and mirrors on all the walls . . ."

"You helped build this?"

"Designed and constructed it. It looks like an old historic home, but we integrated all the modern conveniences and hid them under patchwork quilts and brass beds."

"Sounds wonderful. I can't wait to see it. Murphy, there's so much I have to learn about you. Life is going to be so sweet from now on."

It hurt him more than he was willing to admit. He hadn't quite figured out how to leave her. He had already ruled out just slipping away in the darkness. He owed her more than that. He would try to make her understand and accept.

They checked into the inn. Murphy watched, steeped in pleasure, as she oohed and aahed. It was a mansion. Hardwood floors gleamed, chandeliers sparkled. The smell of furniture wax and candles burning created an old-time feeling.

Turning the key in the lock, he stopped her from walking into the room. Instead, he caught her up in his arms and carried her across the threshold. Her arms twined around his neck and she reveled in the safe, protected, loved feeling his embrace filled her with.

Kicking the door shut, he headed for the huge round bed. Mackensie got the impression of ruffles and flowers. Curtains, bed skirt, rocking chair.

"Wait, please."

He stopped. "I want a bath first. If the tub is as big as you say, we could . . ."

He set her feet on the floor, dropped the suitcase on the bed, and walked over to the bathroom door. Swinging it wide, he bowed at the waist, not without a groan of stiffness, and swept his hand forward. "My lady."

She sighed as she flipped the light switch. It was totally

unbelievable, but there it was. A room, at least twelve by twelve, done in muted pinks and grays. The tub was huge and sparkling, pristine white. Candles lined the edge waiting to be lit. A dressing table sat in the corner. The two sinks were surrounded by miles of marbled countertop. A shower stall took yet another corner. Piles of clean, fluffy towels were stacked on an exposed shelf. The entire room was carpeted. She kicked her shoes off and dug in with her toes.

Time. He realized they had lots of it. He wanted it to be perfect for her. "I'd like to clean up, myself. Why don't you lie down awhile? I'll just borrow your razor and . . ." He picked up the valise.

She moved to him and rubbed her cheek across his bearded face. "Don't take long."

Fierceness darkened his eyes as his need matched her own. He held her tightly to him for a few seconds before closeting himself behind closed doors.

She lay across the big bed and listened as Murphy moved about the bathroom, heard the water rush from the faucet. She pictured him scraping at the growth of hair on his face with her feminine pink razor. She heard the soft spray when he flipped the shower on. His tired, battered body would feel the relief offered by the hot water. He would be leaning into the spray, water droplets rolling over his shoulders, coursing down his torso. . . .

Her hand was tucked beneath her sleepy head. He knelt by the bed and lifted her into his arms. Sleep slipped away. Her eyes opened. A small smile curved her lips as he carried her into the bathroom. When he set her down, she sighed.

Naked, Murphy moved to light the candles. Unable and unwilling to take her eyes off him, she waited until he was bathed in the light before she flipped off the switch. He turned on the water, tested it, and for a moment they just looked at each other.

He moved toward her, slowly. She reached up and began

to unbutton her shirt. He ripped it off. In the dim, flickering candlelight, he freed her from her clothes. Standing only inches away, he waited. She felt her need for him flame up, ready to turn them both to cinders. She stepped forward.

His patience abandoned him. He dragged her to him, crushing her mouth under his. He could never get enough of her. Never. His tongue darted between her lips, to try.

His body was warm and hard and throbbing with energy. She melted to him. Her head fell back and she dropped into a world of only him. Only the feel of his lips, his hands, the sound of his whispered words.

He stepped back, cut the water to the tub, and flipped the switch for the jets. Taking her hand he guided her in. They both slid into the water.

The swirling, pulsating water encompassed them. The candlelight flickered across the walls, across his face. His beautiful face. She drew a hand from under the water to trace it with her fingertips. He kissed them as they moved slowly across his mouth.

"I should have thought to stop and buy wine." His voice was low and just a little rakish.

She grinned. "I'm going to get drunk on you." She moved slowly toward him. Straddling him, she cried out her pleasure as his mouth closed over her breast, as his hand worked magic up her spine.

He left her breast to taste the skin at her waist, her rib cage. She moaned and tilted his face up so she could run her mouth over him. Soothed and delirious, all at once, she nearly floated on top of the churning water.

Smoothing her hands over his shoulders, down across his chest and down, she rejoiced in the feel of him. The tape across his bandage would protect the wound from any further damage.

He took her hands, stopped their roaming, and brought them to his mouth. Turning both palms toward him, he kissed them, ran his tongue the length of her fingers and back.

Mac knew the water was bubbling noisily, but she heard nothing other than the sound of his breathing, his soft expressions of love, felt nothing but his hands and the searing heat that forced her closer and closer to him.

Mackensie knew she had never been to such a beautiful place as his hands and mouth took her. Murphy led her along a path that would only widen and become more beautiful the farther they traveled.

Thomas Justice Murphy came home into a world of complete peace and happiness, and though it was foreign to him, he welcomed it. God, how he appreciated it.

He savored her mouth as she gave and he took. As she gentled him and then roughed him up, as she soothed him and then dared him.

Steam dripped from the walls and clouded the room. Candles flickered. Still the two of them held off, rejoicing in the freedom to explore, to taste, to discover. Through heavy-lidded eyes they watched the pleasure on each other's faces. Through eager hands they searched for the joy, the ecstasy they could find and give to one another. She stilled beneath his hands. He opened his eyes.

Slowly, she lowered herself to meet him. The mere contact nearly sent him over the edge. But he waited, and forced himself to attend to her.

She shuddered. The anticipation of the moment, of knowing one move and she would be filled with him, possessed by him, and he by her, caused her to hold the moment a beat longer.

His eyes leveled on hers. Her heart drew a line to his. His mind locked on hers. Souls swirled to meet, spiraled high and twisted together. She lowered herself, a little at a time. They belonged to each other.

The swirling water, the motion of two humans in love, making love, took them away.

His mouth was eager beneath hers. His hands clasped her hips, driving her down harder. She rested her hands on his chest and felt the distinct rise and fall, the quick jerk of his heartbeat.

No longer could Thomas Justice Murphy control what was happening. He gladly handed himself over to her. She was ready to receive and cherish what he gave her, and make him believe she would adore him and nurture every part of him that he entrusted to her. There was no vulnerability here.

They rode it out. The two of them. His explosion met her implosion and they fused into one. No longer male and female. No longer he or she. Only them. Only now. Only forever.

Eleven

"And for all of you who still resent us,
Remember damn it you're the ones that sent us. . . ."

Mackensie was in her flannel nightgown and Murphy in his jeans. They turned the radio up and the lights down. A slow love song wafted in the air. He took her hand and brought her into his arms. Placing his hand on her back, he led them in a dance.

She looked up into his shadowed face. "The first time we danced together, I expected to be dressed in the finest, with makeup applied just right and my jewelry around my neck to dazzle you."

He kissed the tip of her nose. "You dazzle me. You knock me off my feet. You're beautiful just the way you are."

Her hand rested on his bare shoulder. On tiptoes, she laid her lips to his neck, where his hair curled down. She could feel the stiffness of his jeans through the softness of her gown. She stepped up and put her bare feet on his bare feet and he carried her along as he slowly moved to the music.

They smelled of shampoo and soap, a sharp contrast to the earthy dampness they had lived with for so long. She held tight to him and felt the flame of desire begin to grow again. But she wanted this to go on for a long while— the touching, the holding, the cherishing of two people in love.

He'd remember the way she felt in his arms, the way she smiled up at him with love and respect in her eyes. The way it felt to be joined with her in the act of love. He'd remember. She'd see to it.

There came an uncertain knock on the door. She looked up at him questioningly but he merely smiled and waltzed her over to the door. Opening it, he danced her out of the way. In came four delivery men, each bringing in armloads of baskets overflowing with rose petals in every color imaginable.

When the men looked at him for direction, he merely grinned and said, "Just empty them on the bed."

Mackensie didn't miss the embarrassed exchange of glances between the men as they busied themselves dumping the flower petals across the bed and hurried to depart. She smiled into Murphy's shoulder.

Another man waited outside until the florist's men were on their way out and rolled a cart laden with champagne and midnight snacks past them.

Once the door was closed, Murphy continued the dance as another slow song filled the room. "I don't know which color rose is your favorite."

She looked at the bed that was now covered with white and red, pink and yellow, scarlet and cream. "You're unbelievable. Thank you." The flowers filled the room with their aroma. She breathed deeply and fought back the tears of happiness. He always managed to amaze her.

He danced her toward the bed and slipped the nightgown over her head. Picking her up, he laid her gently on the flowers. The velvety softness caressed her back. The warmth of her body released the sweet aroma even more. She looked up at him and opened her arms.

He stretched full length over her and crushed her against the sheets. He smiled, his lips only a whisper away from hers.

"After all we've been through, it comes back to just you and me. Love me, Murphy."

Sometime during the night, Mackensie woke. The rose petals were on the floor surrounding the bed. Murphy was tossing and turning beside her. Reaching over, she laid her hand on his forehead. His fever had broken during the night. Pulling him into her arms, she held him. After a few moments, he settled.

Later, a scant thread of sunlight streamed through the curtains. She knew she was alone in the big bed without looking. Turning her gaze to the rest of the room, she found him. He had pulled the wooden rocker over to the window and was sitting there, wrapped in the bedspread, staring out the window. She felt the first niggling of fear. What was he thinking? Why had he been so restless all night? It was over. The ordeal was behind them. Only good things waited for them now.

Feeling the chill on her naked body, she got out of bed and walked through the flowers toward him. He heard her and looked up. The smile that covered his face chased any of her doubts away. He opened his arms and the bedspread. She climbed onto his lap.

Cradling her, as one would a child, he held the sleepy Mackensie in his arms and wrapped them both in the bedspread. Her head lolled against his shoulder as he set the rocker into motion and lit a cigarette. Would he really be doing her a favor by leaving her? Yes. She was too kindhearted, too giving to be tied to him. He knew he was an intense man. His emotions ran deep, his pride, his resentments. She would grow weary of struggling along with him. They all had.

"Something was bothering you all night. You were turning over and over. What is it?"

He dodged the question. "Just putting things in order. We have to be at the police station at nine. I need to call my parents."

"What will you tell them?"

He kissed her cheek. "The truth. That my car broke down and I've been waiting for it to be fixed. And you should call your sister. Even though she's been told everything is okay now, she should hear it from you."

He was right. She snuggled closer to him. But she didn't want to think about any of that right now. Not when they were finally free to move about, to laugh and love without fear of being killed. They'd either map out the future or decide to cast it to the wind.

Assuming she would be accompanying him to Florida for a while, she said, "I think I'll just love your parents. After all, if they raised you, they must have the same outlook, same values you have."

His heart did a flip and almost stopped. The reality was all too cold to support his respiratory system. He shivered and she rubbed his arms. "Come back to bed."

"In a little while. For now, let's just stay here. Go back to sleep. I won't let you fall."

Hoping all was as it seemed, she let her eyes close. She fell asleep listening to the steady beat of his heart.

The police station was cold and real compared to the world of soft blankets and the mountainous breakfast they shared at the inn. Phones rang and went unanswered. The hideous tap of computer keys controlled people's lives.

The papers weren't ready. They waited. Murphy became very testy. She soothed him and found that her own patience was wearing thin.

The formalities completed, finally, they walked out into the fresh, chilly late October air. It was nearly noon.

Hand in hand, they walked like high school sweethearts through the parking lot. She felt wonderful. And couldn't quite understand the problem that seemed to distract Murphy. He still wasn't feeling his best. And he had things to straighten out, things to do. That was all, she told herself. She would give him the time he needed. That and everything else, she vowed. Never again would he face anything alone.

When he turned the key in the ignition, he winked at her and she got a glimpse of the Murphy who was in tune with the world. "Where to, lady?"

She threaded her fingers through his. "Back to bed?"

Three days. Mackensie wondered at how quickly they had passed.

He was sleeping beside her on the plush rug in front of the fireplace. Moving easily so as not to wake him, she placed two more logs on the fire and lay back down beside him to watch the play of flame on wood.

She'd never been so happy. They had spent the entire three days just being together. They had taken long walks. Bought cards and played poker with toothpicks. Read the paper to each other and laughed at the news coverage about their ordeal.

In the tub, in the bed, in the rocker in front of the window, on the floor—they had made love over and over. And they had slept late and gone down and eaten huge amounts of food. And they had talked and learned about each other.

But a shadow that surrounded them. When she had asked him about it, he had almost gotten angry and she had not forced the issue. But she would have to go back to Tillery and pack her things. Life had to go on now, and one of the first things she had to do was go back to New York, move her things to storage, and give up the apartment. He hadn't said a word about her going to Florida with him.

They had to talk about what they were going to do. Up until now, they had only danced around it. He wanted what she wanted, didn't he? They were in love. Everyone could see it, even the older lady who ran the inn. She kept calling them newlyweds and lovebirds. Then why did Mac feel so shaky inside? In the morning, in the light of day, she'd find out. Propped up on her elbow, she leaned forward and kissed his chin. Her fingers played music down his chest and further. His eyes slowly opened, a smile dallied at his mouth as he came awake and pulled her to him.

There was no holding back here. Only the acceptance of and the glory in the feelings they could and did bring to each other. Her heart swelled and Mackensie held him tightly.

They rolled together on the floor. Music from the radio played softly in the background. He had her beneath him. His mouth was all over her. Sometimes their lovemaking took on a long, luxurious mood. At others, like now, there was more need. It clawed at them, pushed them furiously together.

Body slid over body, limbs tangled. Her hair, wild and tangled, spread across the floor. He entered her, fast and furiously, taking her quickly to the top. But then he held her there, making her tear at him for more.

Slowly now, he led her along. But she would have none of it. Working her body, trapping him and teasing him, she ran her hands across his back and down his buttocks. Arching up and then down, offering and then promising, giving and then taking, Mackensie increased the tempo.

He sent her over the first peak, soothed her with his hands, and then took her with him, and they soared.

Murphy was surprised to see her fully dressed when he woke up the next morning. They had found their way to the bed last night, and now he lay there watching her pack up the few things they had brought with them.

The time had come and he still hadn't a clue as to how to carry this out. But it had to be done.

Kissing her, he went to the shower. She sat in the rocker and waited for him. She knew something was about to happen that she wouldn't like. Did he not want her? That thought stabbed through her and made her tremble. No, it couldn't be that. She couldn't be so wrong about something so important.

His hair was still dripping. Barefoot and in jeans, he towel-dried his hair and walked toward the dresser.

"Okay, Murphy, what is it?" She rocked quickly, back and forth. "Just say it and we'll figure out what to do about it."

He was brushing his hair back and now his hand stopped in mid-air. Their eyes locked in the mirror.

Lighting a cigarette, he turned and leaned a hip on the dresser. "It's time for me to go."

Although she knew this was more serious than she wanted to hear, she joked. "That's Willie Nelson's song."

He was at her feet, kneeling in front of her. "It's over now, Mackensie. You can go back to New York and pick up your life, change it, do whatever you want."

The fear and betrayal turned to anger. Cold, hard, shocked, and miserable outrage. She watched her knuckles turn white under her grip on the rocker arms. Her head jerked up, her eyes dark with intensity. "Just what the hell does that mean?"

"I'm no good for you."

"Come on. We are good together. You know that. What's this all about? Murphy, this isn't funny."

Angry himself, he stood up and stalked to the window, turning his back to her. "What you feel for me is a combination of things."

"How dare you tell me why I feel the way I do. It was A-okay to drag me into your life, force me to help when you needed someone to get your butt out of trouble." It was the wrong thing to say. She knew it as soon as the words were out of her mouth.

Yes, he had done that. He was relieved to hear the fury in her voice. Had she shed one tear, he wouldn't have been able to say the words that ripped apart his heart. "That's just it," he said, as he continued to stare out the window at nothing. "Think about it. We were thrown together in a situation that was life-threatening. We reacted."

"Reacted!" Standing from the rocker, she faced him. "Turn around, Murphy. Turn around and look at me."

Pure dread stroked his spine. God, he didn't want to do this. He turned, slowly.

"You're not in the army now. You're not fighting a war. Yes, I reacted. I reacted to love. I couldn't love you as much as I do if you didn't love me. As much as you hate to admit it, you need me as much as I need you."

He blew smoke toward the ceiling. "I can't be what you want me to be."

"Whatever you are is what I want you to be."

"I could have just walked off in the night, but I told you I wouldn't. Don't make it so hard for me to do it this way."

Lighting a cigarette of her own, she stalled for time. She realized that the words that were spoken this morning had to be the right words. She had just finished a fight for her life and she was going to finish this fight for their lives.

"I'm not going to let you do it anyway. You want to live the rest of your life with me beside you."

"What I want and what I do are sometimes very different."

"That's wrong."

"Why? Because I know that somewhere down the line, you'll want me to change. I'll start to see it a little here and a little there."

"We've talked about this before, Murphy. I don't want

you to change. I love you just the way you are. I'm not asking for anything different."

"I have to deal with things. Vietnam. Failed relationships. My work. Myself. Society in general. I'm a tough man to be around. I'm a tough man to be."

Her heart broke. He thought she wanted him different. A glimmer of hope eased its way into her heart.

She spoke quietly. "I accept you as you are. I love you, Murphy, just the way you are. Don't walk away from me."

"Don't make promises." He walked from the window to the closet. Whipping a shirt from the hanger, he shoved his arms through. "I don't want promises. They get broken." He pulled his socks and shoes on.

Grinding her cigarette out, she slapped her hand to her hip. "Not my promises. Thomas Justice Murphy, listen to me. I not only love you, I like you. I respect you. I want to be with you for the rest of my life. Anyway you want it. As your wife. As your friend. As your lover. That's the only change that will take place in your life—I'll be there."

He stopped on his way to the door. Turning back toward her, he waited a moment.

She wasn't like anyone else he'd ever met. He wanted her. He could picture her in his cabin, see her in his bed, in his kitchen, in his life. She stood, defiantly, ready to fight for him. It was worth a try. She was worth everything. "It won't be easy."

Oh, God, it's really over. The old life. The new was about to begin. She was so certain, she was willing to gamble her life on it. "I hope to hell it won't."

They were in each other's arms. In one instant and with hardly any movement, they were together. "Trust me, Murphy. Trust me."

"That'll be a first for me."

"And trust yourself." She pulled back a little and looked up at him. "We both have lives to get back in order. Your parents are waiting for you. I have to get back up north and close things up. I'll meet you in two weeks. At the Vietnam Memorial in D.C. Your name is not there, Murphy. I want you to experience it, with me beside you."

She felt the hesitation, but she continued. "November eleventh at eleven o'clock. I think it will be the right place, to begin our journey together."

Mackensie looked up at the man she loved and stood by, waiting.

Trust. That was probably the only word that could have convinced him to try. He wanted her in his life more than he'd ever wanted anything. He'd believe in her as she believed in him. "I have the project to do in San Antonio. You'll like it there. Then I'll take you back to Remington. To the cabin."

"Yes, Murphy. Yes."

New York was cold and bleak and dreary. News of their ordeal had reached the city and the people she worked for showed up at her door. She said her good-byes and arranged to have her things moved to storage. She walked the streets of New York saying farewell to what she had thought she had wanted, and almost ended up with.

There had been no exchange of phone numbers. Whenever fear raised its head to threaten her, she shook it off. He'd be there. She went to the theater alone, to pass the time, and found she couldn't keep her mind on any of it. The days dragged by slowly.

By the time she reached the airport early Thursday morning, she was as anxious as a child before her first trip to a circus. Popping her motion sickness pill down with a soda, she took her place in line. In her carry-on was all she needed to start her new life with Murphy. God, she missed him. She followed the other passengers down the jetway, her heart beating hard in her chest.

Settled in her seat, she was only slightly disappointed

when the pilot announced there would be an insignificant delay due to fog. She forced herself to relax. It would clear soon. The sun would cut through the mist and they would be in the air.

The flight was uneventful. A chatty old man beside her kept trying to divert her thoughts from Murphy. But he didn't succeed. She couldn't wait to be in his arms, to be near him. To see his smile. To hear his voice.

They had to circle the airport because of ground fog. This did fray her nerves. Where was he right now? She checked her watch. It was nine thirty. Oh, God, what if she was late? What would he think? Dear Lord. She panicked. Mackensie forced it away. Trust. She had told him he had to trust. She would, too.

She cursed the fog and forced herself to sit still. If she missed him, she would find him. Virginia wasn't so far away. She'd find him.

As the wheels finally skipped along the runway, Mackensie pulled her carry-on from under the seat in front of her. It seemed to take an eternity to disembark. Almost running through the airport, she found her way to the outside and hailed a cab.

"The Vietnam Memorial. And hurry."

The driver nodded and seemed to think it a little strange that someone would be in a hurry to reach that destination. It certainly wasn't going anywhere. Before long they were behind long lines of cars. He weaved in and out. Mac closed her eyes.

Tipping the driver handsomely for a ride that scared her to death seemed a little frivolous, but she was happy. In a few minutes she would be in his arms, able to look up into that handsome face, and see his smile.

Maybe Veteran's Day was a bad time to meet. Many, many men, women, and children roamed the sidewalk that followed the wall. The light rain still fell, and a ground fog lay across the green grass. She paused by the statue of the three soldiers and looked down at the memorial.

Volunteers were standing behind a podium, taking turns reading the 58,183 names. It crossed her mind that after each name should come the words "I'm sorry." For those who could hear the words, the healing might begin.

It was as she remembered. The weather only added to the bleakness, the sadness. She checked her watch. It was ten minutes to eleven. She scanned the people, almost unidentifiable under umbrellas, coat collars pulled up against the chill, hats on to ward off the rain.

She left the statue of the three soldiers and walked across the wet grass. All the while, her eyes searched the growing crowd for the man she loved. She didn't find him.

It was early yet, she told herself. He lived close enough, so she figured he would drive. He could be slowed by traffic. He could be looking for a parking place right this minute. Again, she doubted her wisdom in choosing this day to meet. She had wanted him to see the throngs of people. She knew it could never make up for all the things that had gone down at the time the guys came home. Never erase the protests and the press. Maybe she had asked too much.

Reaching the wall, she stood behind the rows of people moving along in front of it. She listened to the names. She watched the volunteers, water dripping down their clothes, as they read name after name.

The chill finally got to her and she pulled her collar up and put the carry-on down on the grass so she could shove her hands in her coat pocket. *Come on, Murphy. Come.*

She could literally feel the emotions, the spirits of the men on the wall. One hundred and forty black granite panels. The air was filled with a combination of pride and sadness, loss and memories. There was honor here from each and every man, woman, and child who stood close or walked slowly by. She remembered that it was the most visited memorial in history. Twenty-five million people had filed by, touched the inch-high letters of the names.

Hands would reach out and touch the etched letters. Flowers were set at the foot of the wall, along with small American flags and pictures wrapped in plastic. Crying could be heard above the din of the rain and the reading of the names. Mackensie could make out the heaving shoulders of veterans who found their buddies' names or simply found another veteran standing close by them; wives who found their husbands' names; children, grown now, who found their fathers'. Mackensie felt her own tears coming just as they did the last time, for all of them. For everyone in this country.

It was eleven o'clock. She turned in a full circle, searching faces, watching for new arrivals. Nothing. She shrugged. No big deal. So he's late. He'll be here.

A small band began to assemble on a makeshift platform nearby. The tarp that covered them leaked in several places. She watched. It gave her something to do besides worry.

A souvenir stand stood alone at the end of the walkway. People would stop and look and talk to strangers. They were all here for a common cause on hallowed ground.

The music only added to the solemnity. A small crowd gathered around to listen and show their appreciation. Mackensie studied the faces. So many faces, so many expressions. So much contact between people. Holding hands, shaking hands, hugging, or standing shoulder to shoulder.

Separating herself from the crowd, Mackensie walked to the highest point of ground and watched. And waited.

Eleven fifteen.

Eleven thirty.

She could just hear the strains of the music but she couldn't make out the tune. Still the rain fell and the air grew colder. Her hair was soaked and she began to sniffle. Her feet were cold. Mackensie stood on one foot and then the other, keeping the circulation of blood going and assuring a semblance of warmth.

Eleven thirty-five.

Was that him? She targeted the lone figure that walked past the statue of the three soldiers and paused. He was hunkered into his jacket, his hands were jammed in his pockets. He was too far away for her to be sure. The figure seemed to be looking around. It had to be him.

It might not be him.

She picked up her carry-on and began to walk, tentatively, toward him.

The man was still standing there, looking at the display beyond the field of grass; watching the people file past the wall.

His hair was wet and dark. He was the right size to be Murphy, tall and broad-shouldered, wearing jeans and boots. She walked closer. He had yet to look in her direction. The rain and the mist made it so hard to identify him from this distance.

At that moment, he looked her way. She knew. It was him. Oh, God, it was him. He is here!

Dropping her carry-on, she began to walk faster through the wet grass. He began to walk toward her, through the rain.

"Murphy," she yelled and waved at him. "Murphy."

The lone figure stopped, pulled a hand from his pocket, and saluted her.

She picked up the pace. Her heart beat faster and faster. He's here.

He ran toward her, arms outstretched. She ran, her love for him swelling and growing and nearly spilling out. Now, now when she was so close to him, she could admit the fear that had nearly eaten her alive: that he wouldn't come. But he was here.

She threw open her arms as she got closer. And then she was in his strong arms, being swept up and swung around and around. She heard his laughter, felt the heat of their warm, wet mouths as they came together. Kiss followed kiss. Strangers stopped to watch and smile.

"Thought I wasn't coming, didn't you?" he said against her lips.

"It crossed my mind. But I'd have come looking for you. I love you, Murphy."

"For a minute, I thought about not coming. I don't want a life without you. I'm here. I'm here forever. Mackensie . . . I love you."

It was all she needed. Him and his love. Life would be so good from now on. Rough spots and all. She took his hand and turned to look at the wall.

She asked quietly. "Shall we go down?" They'd come this far.

He followed her gaze and she felt him stiffen. She gave him a few moments, holding tightly to his hand and leaning her head on his shoulder. It had to be his decision.

"Your name isn't there, Murphy."

Without a word, he took the first step forward. They began the walk across the grass toward the black wall slit into the earth. "Will you marry me, Mackensie?"

It was she who stopped this time. Launching herself into his arms, she kissed him and kissed him and kissed him again. "Yes. Yes. Yes."

Her feet on solid ground, once again, they joined hands and continued their journey.

COMING NEXT MONTH

#9 **ALL ABOUT EVE** *by Patty Copeland*
Eve Sutton was just an hour away from her destination when her car sputtered to a halt. And a stranded tourist was the very last thing Dr. Adam Wagner needed.

#10 **THE CANDY DAD** *by Pat Pritchard*
A down-to-earth single suburban mom was hardly his type but Jesse Daniels couldn't deny the sweet fantasies Rennie Sawyer inspired.

#11 **BROKEN VOWS** *by Stephanie Daniels*
When Wendy Valdez' smile melted his heart, Jack O'Connor didn't know how to respond. It would be easy to fall—fast and hard—for this tempting woman.

#12 **SILENT SONG** *by Leslie Knowles*
Nicole Michael couldn't believe it was him. Had Jake Cameron discovered the reason she'd left him so abruptly?

Plus four other great romances!

AVAILABLE THIS MONTH:

#1 **PERFECT MATCH**
Pamela Toth

#2 **KONA BREEZE**
Darcy Rice

#3 **ROSE AMONG THORNES**
Pamela Macaluso

#4 **CITY GIRL**
Mary Lynn Dille

#5 **SILKE**
Lacey Dancer

#6 **VETERAN'S DAY**
GeorgeAnn Jansson

#7 **EVERYTHING ABOUT HIM**
Patricia Lynn

#8 **A HIGHER POWER**
Teresa Francis